# *Ruin*

*Beppe Fenoglio*

# *Ruin*

*Translated by John Shepley*

*The Marlboro Press*

First English language edition.


Originally published in Italian under the title
LA MALORA


The publication of the present volume has been made possible in part by a grant from the National Endowment for the Arts.

Manufactured in the United States of America.

Library of Congress Catalog Card Number 92-80362

Coth: ISBN 0-910395-83-7
Paper: ISBN 0-910395-84-5

## *Translator's Note*

This story takes place in Piedmont in northwestern Italy, in the range of hills known as Le Langhe. As the reader will see, the inhabitants of this area tend to define themselves according to the particular *langa* on which they happen to live.

# Ruin

It was raining all over the *langhe*, and up in San Benedetto my father was getting wet underground for the first time.

He'd died on the Thursday night before, and we buried him on Sunday, between the two masses. It was a good thing my master had advanced me three napoleons, otherwise there was nothing in our whole house to pay for the priests and the coffin and the meal for the relatives. The stone we'd put for him later, when we were able to hold our heads up.

I started back on Wednesday morning. My mother wanted to pack my share of our father's clothes in my bundle, but I told her to put them aside for me, I'd pick them up the next time Tobia gave me some time off.

Well, as I was walking along the road, I felt calm and relieved. My brother Emilio, who was studying to be a priest, would have been happy and reassured if he'd known how resigned I felt inside. But the moment that from the height of Benevello I saw Tobia's farm on the lower *langa*, all my resignation left me. Here I'd just buried my father and already I was going back to take up my whole miserable life again, and not even his death could do anything to change my fate. And I was ready to turn right, go down to the Belbo, and look for a spot deep enough to drown myself.

Instead I kept going, because right away I thought of my mother, who's never had any luck, and my brother, who'd gone back to the seminary with a life sentence like my own.

I stopped at the tavern in Manera, not so much to rest but so as not to arrive at the Pavaglione in time to be given any work to do—I might have said or done something awful.

Tobia and his family treated me like a sick man, but only for one day. Next day Tobia came down on me hard, and by the time it got dark I felt as though I'd never done such a day's work in my life. It did me good. A little the way it does you good when you've worked all night binding sheaves in the heavy dew, and instead of going to bed you start scything again as the sun comes up.

How my family had sunk to the point of sending me, a son, to be a bond servant far from home is something maybe I'm still not old enough to understand. Our father and mother no more explained their affairs to us than they would have explained how they'd made us get born. Without ever saying a word, they set in front of us work, food, a few pennies on Sunday, and finally, for me, going away to be a bond servant.

We weren't the poorest of our relatives and all of them

got along pretty well. Some had a store, some a butcher shop, some a good piece of land of their own. Besides, we'd seen how they all came for our father's funeral driving a horse, and not one of them on foot like a beggar.

We must have felt fairly strong if, when I was about eight years old, my parents tried to buy the store in San Benedetto. The Canonica family got it instead, with money they'd borrowed from Norina of the post office. Our father was too afraid of going into debt at that time.

Now it's clear to me that our father didn't much care anymore about working the land and already saw himself going with horse and wagon to the markets of Alba and Ceva to buy supplies for his store, and when instead he had to go back to stooping over the soil, he'd lost a lot of will power and perseverance. We boys kept working the same as before, though he gave us fewer orders and checked up on us less often, but at noon and at supper we always found less polenta and almost no more Robiola cheese on the table. And at Christmas we didn't see dried figs anymore, much less tangerines.

Our mother doubled her production of ripened cheese, but she wouldn't let us touch even the bits and pieces on the edge of the basin. And when she heard that in Niella they were paying one soldo more per round than in our village, she went to sell it in Niella, and when later she found out they were paying a little better in Murazzano, she climbed two hills to go and sell it up there. It wasn't long before she became like our father's older sister, always out of breath, her eyes either too bright or too dull, never the way they should be, her face all pale and with red spots, as though at every moment she'd just run all the way uphill from the Belbo to our house. When we weren't there, she prayed and talked to herself out loud—once when I came in from the fields for a moment, I found her curdling the milk and saying, "If only I had that daughter now!" She was talking about our sister, who was born after Stefano and died from some kind of brain sickness before I was born. They'd named her Giulia, after our grandmother in Monesiglio, and I don't know about Stefano, but Emilio and I didn't miss her. But even then I was like an owner walking past his land when I walked by the cemetery, and never looked the other way.

Things were going badly: you could tell by the amount of food we had and the way we skimped on wood, so that every time I saw our mother take out some money and count it in her hand before spending it, I trembled, I really did, as though I expected to see an arch fall down when you take away a stone. It got to the point where to save matches on fall and winter evenings, we'd send Emilio over to the nearest farmhouse to get the lamp lit. I went only once, one evening when Emilio had a fever, and the family at the Monastero lit the lamp for me, but the old woman said, "Go back and tell your folks that one of these days we're going to bring our lamp over to you, and you'll have to use one of your matches."

Our father sold half the woodyard along with the meadow we had beside the Belbo, but the money from those sales didn't do us much good. Almost all of it went to pay taxes and to keep the Canonicas happy so they wouldn't cut off our credit at the store. It was then that our parents went into debt with the old schoolmistress

Fresia for those hundred lire that later decided the fate of my brother Emilio.

To ask God's help in keeping our heads above water, our mother one year made a pilgrimage to the shrine of the Madonna del Deserto, which is a long way off, on a mountain where the sea is supposed to be right there on the other side. I remember like it was yesterday. We'd been standing in the fields for a while watching a procession of women on the Mombarcaro road, when out of the house comes our mother in her Sunday best, and with a little package of food. Our father was right behind her, yelling, "You old whore, you're not going off with that bunch of good-for-nothing bitches?" She turned around but without stopping and only to look him in the eyes. And he still behind her, and starting to run so as to be sure of catching her. And meanwhile he was saying, "Who knows how many days it'll be before you get back, with your feet all swollen and your body so worn out you won't be any good to me for a week." Then she stopped and said to him, "Let me go, Braida. I haven't been out of this house for seven years. Let me go, it's for the good of my soul."

"Your soul can fly!" he yelled in her face. But then he said, "Have a good time, old woman. Did you at least leave us something to eat?"

She was able to leave, and in a little while we saw her catch up with the procession. She stepped right along and soon was near the head of the line, and you could see not only from the way she walked that she was serious about it, but also because she didn't turn around and look for company, while all the others were walking as though they were out for a stroll. Four days later, she came back in the night, and next morning she got up at her usual hour and did her everyday work. But it didn't do any good, God was never on our side.

Then the king called Stefano to be a soldier, he went to report and drew a low number. Our father cursed, our mother cried, but Stefano himself was glad. I heard him that evening, when I was in the pasture near the Belbo, where he was bathing stark naked and yelling with joy, but wild yells that scared me and the sheep. Well, he stayed at home another two months, and on Saturdays would go with his fellow conscripts to make the rounds of the taverns on our *langa* and not come back until Monday night, so drunk we had to throw him in the stable. And then he left, one night while Emilio and I were still asleep.

He wrote to us, and we read that he was in the artillery and stationed in Oneglia. I didn't know anything about that town except that it was on the seashore, and I kept waiting for him to come home on leave so I could ask him what the sea was like. But Stefano didn't come home on leave, he only sent a photograph of himself, and to see it you had to go in the old folks' bedroom, where it was hanging by a string among the olive sprigs and church candles. He wrote us once that he wasn't one of those soldiers who sweat it out marching and training, he was smarter and had got himself a post as an officer's orderly and was doing just fine. So our parents had Emilio take up his pen and write Stefano to send us some money since he was doing so well. After that letter he never wrote us again, we didn't get a penny from him, and he never came home on leave. At home we weren't able to knock off so much as one scudo from the debt to the schoolmistress.

They released him after twenty-one months. He'd got brawnier and more stuck-up, it took him a whole month to get used to the work again and pitch in. Now he'd go to the tavern every evening, and many nights he came home drunk from the wine they stood him in exchange for the stories he told. With us, his brothers, he didn't seem to feel like talking about the sea and the places he'd been, but at the tavern he always had a crowd around him and all he talked about was foreign women, which was disgusting. He had gone back to plowing with me behind the animals, while Emilio led them but I whose arms were half the size of his did twice as much work. Every five minutes he'd straighten up and often looked toward the Bossola pass.

With Stefano back in the family, it came time for Emilio to leave—he was going to the seminary in Alba to study to be a priest. We'd been able to pay the schoolmistress a couple of scudi more or less, and she, finding herself with one foot in the grave and with no need to have her hundred lire back, came one evening to tell our parents that she'd cancel the debt if we sent our Emilio to become a priest. Not only would she cancel the debt, but she'd contribute one scudo a month for his board at the seminary and get the parish priest to come up with another lira or two.

Emilio said nothing, just as I said nothing in front of Tobia Rabino when he became my master. The old folks said yes fast enough.

The reason for it may even have offended our Lord, but

all the same my brother Emilio was doing the right thing in becoming a priest. First of all because he was a good boy, the best in church and the one who spent the most time there, and besides that he was the smartest in school in all San Benedetto, and because he was the most innocent he was the one my folks told to pray when they had something they wanted to ask for from heaven. Also he wasn't very strong, the only thing he could do without straining too much was to lead the animals.

He left for the seminary one Saturday morning. Canonica, who was on his way to the market in Alba, took him in his cart. We all kissed him on the cheeks before he got in. Our mother cried, and our father called her names because she was crying and said, "You stupid woman, when I'm not around anymore, can you think of anything better than going to live with him where he'll be a priest and keeping house for him?" There was Stefano, and I couldn't believe that in five minutes I'd be back in the fields without Emilio close by anymore, and there was Fresia, the schoolmistress, talking Italian to Emilio. The priest wasn't there, but Emilio had been to the rectory the night before to hear how he ought to behave when he got to the seminary.

Canonica didn't dare say giddap to the horse because he could hear my mother crying. The schoolmistress went over to her and said, "But, Melina, just think what a consolation it will be when he says his first mass. And you'll be the first to receive the host from him." Then our father made a sign to Canonica and they left. If anyone had told me I'd see him before a year had gone by, and there in Alba, where I'd be going with my master Tobia, I wouldn't have believed it.

I was about to turn seventeen, and even with the shortage of food in our house, I was so big-boned that I weighed seventy kilos. When I went to sleep that night, I knew that next day our father was going to the market in Niella, but by himself, which is why his voice gave me a jolt just when it was getting light: "Agostino, get up and put on your Sunday clothes." I won't say for sure that I saw what was coming—it all happened as though I were a lamb at Easter.

I used to like going to the markets, and it was at a market that I received my life sentence. It didn't happen right away, I was able to walk around the Niella market as I pleased, and more than once I ran into the man from the lower *langa* who one hour later would be feeling my arms and measuring the width of my shoulders and then haggling with my father over how much I was worth.

"I'll pay you seven napoleons a year for him," Tobia Rabino said.

"That comes to one napoleon for every ten kilos he weighs," said my father.

All I could think, in the middle of all those words, was that my mother at home knew about it, and it was as though she was there with us in the Niella market. It seemed to me that my father and Tobia were trying to see which one could yell the louder, and the louder voice was my father's.

They shook hands. "If I'm satisfied with him," Tobia said, "I'll give him a pair of pants every Christmas he spends in my house. But don't count on it right away, it's not part of the deal."

"And make him work!" my father yelled after him, but this wasn't cruelty toward me, only a challenge to that man from the lower *langa* to see if with hard work he could break someone from the Braida clan.

A week later I left on foot for the Pavaglione. Tobia had told me how to get there. In my veins I could feel the blood of others who had been bond servants.

For almost three years I stayed at the Pavaglione, and now it's five months since I left it, but to me it seems like yesterday evening that I got there for the first time, and while the dog kept up its barking Tobia came to meet me on the threshing floor, and as he greeted me he felt my arms and shoulders to make sure that in that week my folks hadn't let me waste away on purpose.

The one I can't really complain about is Tobia's wife. I saw right away that she had a nice face and she took a liking to me and always treated me well. Never once did she cut her sons' hair without then using the bowl and scissors on me, and many winter nights, after calling the dog and chaining him up to a tree, she came in the stable with the lamp to see if I had enough covers. And she took even better care of me when she found out I had a brother who was studying to be a priest. I called Tobia by his name, but I always called her mistress.

She and Tobia had three children. The oldest was named Ginotta, and I didn't know her very well because she got married and left when I'd been in their house only six months—two marriage brokers were already coming up to the Pavaglione for her at the time I arrived. I didn't get to know Ginotta very well, but it was by living around her for that short time that I got an idea of what that sister of ours might have been been able to do for our family if she'd lived, and I'm sure that it wouldn't have been any different.

One of the two boys was a little older than me and the other a little younger. I hardly said more than a couple of words to either one of them every day, but neither of the two ever tried to lord it over me, maybe because they knew it wouldn't take more than an angry outburst and a little calculation in their father's head to send both of them to the same fate as mine far away from home. In fact, Tobia would sometimes order them to do some job or other while I was just standing around, and they did it without even thinking of passing it on to me.

To get to Tobia, he always treated me the same as he did his sons. He made me work just as hard and gave me the same amount to eat. Under Tobia, you not only worked your hide off but a little more besides—you had to keep up with the three of them and they pulled like three steers under one yoke. If only what we were given to eat had matched all that toil, but a normal meal at Tobia's was like what we ate at my house on the darkest days. At noon and at supper it was almost always polenta, and to give it a little flavor we took turns rubbing it with an anchovy that hung by a string from the rafter. It didn't look much like an anchovy anymore, but we still kept rubbing for a few days, and the one who rubbed more than was fair was Ginotta, who was supposed to get married soon. Tobia whacked her across the table, whacked her with one hand while with the other he stopped the anchovy from bouncing around on its string.

After these suppers, Tobia wanted everyone to sing. He blew out the lamp and ordered his sons and daughter to sing. They sang, and even in the dark you could guess that Tobia was smiling like someone was stroking his fur. I couldn't join in because I didn't know any of their songs, but later I learned them all because that's what Tobia wanted. He ordered me to do it the same way he ordered me to work in the fields.

Lots of times, lying on my straw mattress in the stable, and waiting for my stomach to fall asleep so that my head could fall asleep too, I wondered if there wasn't a danger of not getting those seven napoleons at the end of my year. And I also thought about Ginotta, who suffered from the same hunger as the rest of us, and already looked as though she'd been married for a year.

I soon found out why they were working like such demons and tightening their belts so much, from a conversation between Tobia and his older son behind the house. I was there by myself, looking at the slope of Sant'Elena and waiting for them to call me from inside to come and eat, when Tobia and his son Jano came around the house. They squatted on their heels, the old man spat on the ground, the son spat on his father's spit, Tobia spat again and so did Jano.

"We've reached a good point, Jano," Tobia said.

"But you've been saying that ever since I was born!"

"I'm telling you that now we've reached a good point."

"And for when will it be?"

"You must be almost nineteen now. Well, when that glorious day comes, you still won't be a man."

"But I'm a man already!"

Tobia burst out laughing. "Sure, you're a man already. You're not my son, you're my lawyer. Listen to what I have in mind." But just then the mistress put her hands to the grating of the kitchen window and called us to come in and eat. "Wait, whore," Tobia yelled back at her. "We men are having a talk." And then he said to Jano: "I have in mind a dozen *giornate*,* no more, but all of them facing south, half for grain and half for vineyards. With a woodyard and also a meadow to keep a couple of sheep and a mule. To fertilize it we can use the ashes from the stove."

"And where would this land be?"

Tobia raised himself on his knees to let a fart more comfortably and then settled back. "Not here, not on this shitty *langa* that kills you just climbing it even before you work it. I'm thinking of one of those sunny little hills right above Alba, where the snow melts as soon as it falls."

That's how I found out about the Rabinos' plans, and it only made me feel worse. I wouldn't have minded so much working like a slave if it was just to help them dodge hunger and cold, but that they should work my hide off to get rich while at home we were losing our daily bread from one meal to the next, this was something that made me envious and poisoned my labors.

* From *giorno*, day. An old measure of land in Piedmont (3810 square meters), supposedly the area that a pair of oxen could plow in one day. (Tr.)

In carrying out his plan Tobia didn't spare anyone anything, and that's for sure. One day he and I took the cart and went down to the mill at Trezzo. On the way back, he surprised me when we were still pretty far from home by coming up alongside me and saying, "Go back by yourself, by now you know the way." He went on ahead at a pace that I could never have kept up with. When I got back to the Pavaglione on my own and stopped the cart at the gate, the two sons and the daughter were there on the threshing floor, staring so hard at the door of the kitchen that they didn't even notice me. On the threshing floor and in the house there was complete silence, except for the swish of the strap in the air and the sound of it hitting the mistress's back. Then Tobia came out with the strap still in his hand, walked up to his sons and daughter, and started hitting them with the strap. "I hope it rots your guts!" he yelled at every blow, "I hope it rots your guts!"—until his voice gave out but not his arm. Well, none of the three flinched or cried out, not even Ginotta. They'd been eating rabbit while we were down there at the mill, and Tobia had arrived in time to catch them with only the bones.

The owner of the Pavaglione was, and probably still is, a man in Alba, who had the finest pharmacy in town. Even Tobia sometimes boasted that his boss had the best pharmacy of any in Alba, and yet whenever he mentioned him he called him a shithead and wished he'd drop dead. He moaned and groaned about always having him on his neck, and this sounded strange to me because in the whole first year I spent at the Pavaglione I only saw the owner twice—once down in Alba when we took him an accounting of his share, and another time when he drove up in a gig with a lawyer friend of his, who was also from Alba. It was February, and they'd made a bet as to whether the snow would come first to the Pavaglione or to that lawyer's farm. After taking a look around, they stopped to have lunch. The mistress brought out bread and wine and four Robiola cheeses, one on top of another, and they cut little pieces out of all of them to see which was the most tasty but then ended by nibbling on all four. The rest of us out of surprise had stopped working in the stable, where we were making nests for the hens, and were standing and watching in the door of the kitchen, with our eyes popping out of our heads. As soon as they'd left in their fine gig, Tobia planted himself in the middle of the threshing floor and started cursing so furiously that after a while I had to get away from him, and the mistress went up and shook him by the shoulder. "That's enough, Tobia," she said, "aren't you ashamed?"

"Ah, so now I need a woman to teach me shame!"

"Be a little more Christian, look around you once in a while. You curse in this disgusting way because the landlord comes to see you once in a blue moon. But turn around and look at those people at the Serra, whose landlord doesn't own a business in town and so they've got him underfoot in the fields and vineyards for months at a time."

And Tobia: "Listen to her, worrying about those people at the Serra. Worry about your own family, whore, because we need it more than you know, with a landlord who for no reason at all comes up and eats four cheeses on us at a time!" And he started cursing again, just to upset her more.

After supper I heard the mistress say to her daughter, "Do you have your kerchief, Ginotta? We'd better go, both of us, and say a prayer at Cappelletto. If we don't ask the Lord to forgive him, something terrible could happen tonight, to us or to the fields."

Tobia stood right in the doorway, making it hard for them to pass, but then he moved aside and called after them: "I didn't hear any church bells, you two whores!"

After I'd been working for months at the Pavaglione, I got a chance to go down to Alba. I was so eager to go that I hardly got any sleep that night, and all it took to wake me up at daybreak was the noise Tobia made when he opened the box of the cart to put inside it the bread and lard and the pint of wine for us to eat and drink down there in town.

Down we went, Tobia behind the brake and I leading the animal, and at every turn I expected to see Alba spread out before my eyes like a brightly colored map. Whenever in San Benedetto we talked about cities, we always meant Alba, and anyone who'd never seen one and wanted to picture what it looked like tried to picture Alba. Well, this time I would see it and walk in it, and even if it was for the first and last time, I'd still be able to take part in any conversation about Alba and never again have to envy those who'd seen it and acted high and mighty when they talked about it. And though I'd be far away from home when I saw Alba, in a certain sense I was going home, because that's where my brother Emilio was.

There was no need for Tobia to yell in my ears to look at Alba because my eyes were already full of it, and it hit me so hard that I let go of the animal and went to the edge of the road to get a better look. I fixed in my head the steeples and towers and the blocks of houses, and then the bridge and the river, more water than I'd ever seen, but so far away in the plain that I could only imagine the sound of the current—that Tanaro River in which, the story goes, so many of our breed from the *langhe* have thrown themselves to end it all.

Tobia took hold of my shoulders as though aiming me and said, "You see that big palace with the garden in front of it and all those arches on the first floor? That's where your brother is studying to be a priest."

I was now more impatient than ever to get there, but first the hooves of our animal had to strike sparks down below on the pavements of Alba.

It was early morning, but already I saw so many people walking around, men, women, children, and even soldiers, that I didn't realize that each one had a first and last name like we do up in the *langhe*. I looked at everything and everybody, so as not to miss anything, and I felt strange because nobody looked at me. But there was one thing I couldn't do, and that was to look in the face the fellows in Alba who at first sight seemed to be my age. I'd see them coming but when our paths crossed it was too much for me, I had to lower my eyes, and then turn around and look at them once they'd gone by. Until a rage came over me almost like hatred, and looking at their backs I said to myself: "Ah, if only we were on the *langa*, I'd beat the hell out of you one by one, if we were on my territory." It's a sad way to think, but that's what I was like in those days.

We went to where our landlord lived, a beautiful big house standing all by itself on an avenue. To go in the courtyard you passed under an arch.

There were already two carts lined up in the middle of the courtyard, they were the tenants from that landlord's other two farms, and while I was turning our cart around they greeted Tobia: "Hey, you from the Pavaglione." And Tobia: "Hey, you from the Commanda, hey, you from the Rombone." But all three of them in low voices, because they knew the landlord was still sleeping. I lined the cart up with the others and then took a look at the other bond servants. They were adjusting their loads and the yokes on their animals, so I thought I ought to do the same, and without asking Tobia I started doing it. But Tobia glanced at me and said, "Don't touch anything, anyway it won't make any difference. He's got it in for me and if I brought him gold he'd say it was brass."

A girl came out on the terrace, she must have been the landlord's maid. She walked up and down the terrace a couple of times, looking at us in a snooty way, then turned her head and went back in the house. "That whore," said Tobia. "Look how she behaves. She's one of us, I know she was born and raised in a pigsty in Benevello, but after two years of being a bondmaid in Alba, look how she behaves."

Then the landlord came out. He was wearing a long

yellow robe like I'd never seen a man wear, and his face looked as though he'd got up on the wrong side of the bed. Without leaning forward he looked down at the carts and right away yelled, "Tobia, you dumb prick, is that the way to load a cart? And look how you've harnessed that animal! You murderer, do you think the animals belong only to you?"

I held my breath and looked sideways at Tobia. His head was slumped on his chest and his jaws moved as though he were chewing his tongue. I saw that even the other tenants, who didn't come into it, also hung their heads. The landlord came down just as he was into the courtyard and started asking his tenants questions in a corner, and there too Tobia got the worst of it. Then the tenants came back to us and made us turn the animals around, because we had to go and unload at a mill where the landlord had told them.

Afterwards Tobia was cheerful and seemed anxious that I be cheerful too, but I didn't feel like raising my eyes and looking him in the face. I kept wondering if up there at the Pavaglione they knew how the landlord treated their Tobia down here in Alba.

We parked cart and animal at a public stable where Tobia was known and ate sitting on a flight of steps, without saying a word, like the friars. I swallowed my food without tasting it, I was so eager to run and see Emilio in his new condition. Tobia understood and let me go—we were to meet back here in four hours.

"How do I get to the seminary?"

"Ask along the way. And don't be afraid to speak to these city folks. They're animals just like us."

I started out, and asked two people in the street where the seminary was. Each one told me only partly how to get there, but the third just turned around and pointed at a building that must really be ancient, right there behind us.

I went in the entrance way. At the end was a big door but it was closed, and to the left a small door, half open. I stuck my head in and sure enough it was the visitors' room. There were groups of people standing around a boy dressed in black or a young man already with his red buttons, and on the benches along the wall people sitting and waiting and looking at their dusty shoes. They all spoke in low voices and no one laughed, as though they were visiting a hospital. Of all those people, not one had the accent of the *langhe*.

An old man came limping up to me and asked me who I was looking for.

"My brother is studying here. His name is Emilio Braida." I wanted to add that he was from San Benedetto, but the old man must have known enough about him already because he turned his back on me and went out a little door at the end.

Emilio would be coming in from there, and I shifted my feet on the floor as though I were expecting a shock and had to brace myself for it. Then he came in: he was still wearing the same black suit that he'd left in, and his face looked as though for him the sun had stopped rising. We kissed each other on the cheeks and right away Emilio said something I didn't catch, because it was strange to hear his voice, it had changed so much.

"I've come down to Alba with my master," I told him. "I'm not at home anymore, you know."

"They wrote me about it right away."

"They write to you? What do they say? Do you have a letter you can show me?"

"They haven't written to me in a long time. But I've written to them, and if they don't answer soon I'm going to write a letter to the priest."

"So tell them you've seen me and that I'm all right. Next time I come, it would be nice if you could show me a letter from home."

Every minute a bell rang from inside, and each time Emilio pricked up his ears.

"But you look awfully pale, Emilio."

"They almost never let us out of here." Then his voice sank to a whisper: "Agostino, have you got any money on you?"

I had ten soldi and took them out. "You want them? Anyway I'd just lose them at *nove*."*

"I'm hungry, Agostino. Take that money and go out and buy me something to eat."

"What should I buy you?" Of course, I remembered what Emilio liked to eat, but in the old days at home. Now I felt as though I should even ask him how he breathed.

"Buy me anything."

I didn't start right away, I just stood there with my ten soldi in my hand, and in my brother's eyes I saw as in a

* A card game. (Tr.)

mirror the two of us in the village, one Sunday afternoon when we'd been catching crayfish by hand in the Belbo. "Buy me something that'll cheer me up"—and he touched me on the arm to wake me up and get me started. And when I was already at the door, he ran after me and told me to buy him some apple compote.

In a store there in the food market I bought him four soldi worth of apple compote and six of pickled fish. I went back with the two little packages, but the door of the waiting room was closed and there was no sound from inside. I got frantic, which made me knock pretty hard, but at least five minutes went by before I heard the lame man coming. He opened the door and said, "They're all in chapel now. What's that you're holding in your hand?"

"Something to eat that my brother asked for."

"Give it to me and I'll give it to him"—and like a fool I found myself with empty hands and the wood of the door against my nose.

There was nothing to do but go away. When I got outside, I turned around to look up at the front of the seminary, and I even took a few steps up an alleyway that ran alongside the building, as though looking for a hole through which I could see my brother again. That solid stone made me want to call out loud to our mother, for both of us.

I went back to the stable. I had no idea what time it was, there were only about half as many people walking around, and a wind had sprung up that smelled of rotting grass and frogs. I don't know how I found my way. Tobia wasn't there yet, which made my heart start beating faster, and to make it pass I went up to the animal and put my arm against its dewlap. I wanted to be at the Pavaglione, I felt it was my home, and I was sure that Emilio would have been glad to be there too.

Then Tobia showed up, carrying his wife's shopping basket full of things, and away we went.

Nothing else out of the ordinary happened, except that Ginotta got married. The rest of us kept dreaming of that day because for once we'd be able to stretch our legs under a table that would be worth it. Like everybody on that *langa*, I took Amabile to be Ginotta's man. In fact, her family had sent away the marriage broker for the one in Agliano and now it was only Amabile's broker who turned up at the Pavaglione, but these were his last visits. There had already been a little celebration, and after mass Amabile had walked in front of us with Ginotta from the church to the crossroads of the Pavaglione, and that evening when we came back from watching the football game at Cappelletto, Ginotta made sure to ask whether Amabile had won or lost, because he was the captain of one of the teams.

All that was left was for the broker to come up there with Amabile's family to set the date of the marriage and the day to go down to Alba to buy Ginotta the shoes and the wedding ring, and then stop by to tell the landlord and see if he'd give a present. Instead, one Saturday evening, when Tobia had left the lamp lit for Ginotta so that she could make a list of the things she was taking so that her mother would have a record of it, that Saturday evening the marriage broker arrived by himself when no one was expecting him.

"Something's got screwed up," said Tobia, and without inviting the broker to sit down, told him to speak up right away.

"Don't get mad, Rabino, but my client wants you to add an extra napoleon."

We were all expecting Tobia to explode with rage, and instead he found a reasonable voice and spoke like a lawyer. He said, "Has Amabile considered the fact that he owns his own land while I'm just a tenant? And yet I'm giving him my daughter, she's healthy, not at all bad-looking, and still just the way she came out of her mother, and I've put up a dowry of four napoleons. What more can Amabile ask? Let's hear it."

"He says you're a big tenant, while the land he owns is no bigger than a handkerchief and by no means the best."

Tobia was holding his jaws in his hands and rubbing his white stubble, but before he found an answer, Ginotta butted in, and I'd never seen her so firm.

"Tell it to *me*," she said to the broker. "Is Amabile really set on that extra napoleon?"

"From what he's told me, yes."

"So Amabile's set on one napoleon, he who'll bet a scudo in a five-game football match! Well, Amabile's not worth that extra napoleon. I'm sorry for you, for having to come all this way and all the talk you've wasted, I'm sorry you should lose the overcoat you would have earned, but your Amabile's not worth that extra napoleon. As far as I'm concerned, the contract is broken."

Tears came to the marriage broker's eyes, he stood there for a moment with his mouth open and his hands clasped, looking into our faces one by one, even at me who had nothing to do with it, and meanwhile Ginotta took her mother outside to consult with her. Then the broker got his speech back, and with his hands still clasped he started begging Tobia, saying how he had always spoken well of him to everyone since the first day that Tobia had come as a tenant farmer to take over the Pavaglione, that now through no fault of his own he was in danger of being a laughingstock and all his marriage deals would be ruined, and that it must simply be a bad evening, because Ginotta was the most good-natured girl about whom he'd ever negotiated.

"You heard my daughter," said Tobia. "How can you ask me to overrule her, a daughter so devoted to her father that she won't let him throw money away on her?"

That was it, they went on talking some more, and I can't remember all the arguments, but the broker wasn't able to get anywhere with Tobia, and when he left he was crying like a baby, with no hope left. No sooner was he gone than Ginotta came back in. "My mother and I agree," she told her father. "If you have nothing against it, you can send for the broker who speaks in the name of that man in Agliano."

I ran the errand for them myself, all the way to the Badellinis, but on the evening he was supposed to come, he was late, and suddenly we heard the sound of a beating and calls for help down on the road to Mango, while our dog kept barking until all his fellow watchdogs had joined in. We men ran down to help, but when we got to the Mango road there was no one but the marriage broker, all doubled up from the beating and covering his face with his hands.

"I'm spitting blood," he said. "It was Amabile's people, out of jealousy. Just remember, Tobia, what I've gone through for the sake of your daughter."

But Tobia just told him that next time he'd better come by way of Mompiano.

Things went ahead fast and to Tobia's satisfaction. Four napoleons were enough for that man in Agliano, and as for the bride, he had such trust in the marriage broker and his description that he would wait to see Ginotta until when they were standing next to each other in front of the priest. Tobia, however, took two days to go and look at his son-in-law's property, and came back saying there wasn't much land but all of it was planted with new vines and tilled by an expert.

There were just two more days until the wedding, and the mistress started preparing the meal. She really would have liked Tobia to send for a cook in Treiso who was well known for her wedding banquets, but Tobia said he'd already spent too much money on just the regular things. So the dinner was prepared by the mistress and Ginotta. On the day before they wouldn't even let us in the kitchen for fear we'd sample the dishes and also to keep it a surprise—that day we ate on the porch from bowls that Ginotta brought out to us, pulling the door closed behind her with her foot. But on our way back to the fields, we went around the house to see what the mistress had thrown away. We found feathers and chicken guts and that made us happy.

They got married in Trezzo at the end of October. The

bridegroom no longer had his mother and came with his father, his brother, and an uncle in the marriage broker's wagon. They all made a good enough impression.

More people came on Tobia's side than I expected—a brother of his and two sisters with their husbands and children. They brought their presents to Ginotta in shoe boxes. I was worried, and it spoiled the ceremony for me down in Trezzo, worried that with so many guests there wouldn't be room at the table for me, who wasn't a relative but only a bond servant, and that they'd stick me in some hole where they might even forget about me sometimes. But they squeezed together and let me sit at the table, among the children.

I'd never eaten such a meal before, and even now it would be a good day for me if I were to get invited to one like it. The mistress didn't hold back on me and every time she heaped something in my plate, she'd say, "Eat, Agostino, eat, boy. You're not a member of the family and so you don't have to pay any attention to their conversation, just eat and don't waste time." And in fact I wasn't paying any attention, but after a while when we were well along in the meal, I heard Tobia's voice sink lower and lower and then break when he started crying. We all stopped chewing and just sat there and the mistress asked him what was the matter.

"Nothing," said Tobia's older sister, "it's just the wine, it's affected his heart."

"Yes, yes," said the other sister, "it must be the wine, it's gone to his head."

"What can we do? What do you want us to do for you, Tobia?"

"Nothing at all, leave him alone," said the first sister, and in fact in the silence Tobia got control of himself, but didn't give any explanation.

There were times when I had to stop eating for a moment, and then I'd look at Ginotta sitting next to her brand-new husband, and though I was full of food and wine I couldn't help thinking that in a few hours she'd be gone for good, and that for me the Pavaglione would then become worse than ever. But actually the food and wine kept me from feeling too sad about it.

As fate would have it, Tobia had to disturb everything at that wonderful banquet. All of a sudden, he said loudly that he had to go out and take a piss, and he got up and went outside, making everybody move. In less than a minute we heard him cry out, and as soon as we could get ourselves untangled from the chairs and each other we ran to the threshing floor, but we found him and picked him up at the bottom of the incline. He'd gone to the edge to make water and since he had more of it in his head than in his feet, he'd fallen over like a pole. It looked like he'd broken his nose, and his face was covered with blood and with dirt that he himself had wetted. His older sister felt his forehead and said he already had a fever. We put him to bed and went back to finish the meal.

We got up when the church bell at Cappelletto rang for vespers, and we were all heavier than lead. Ginotta wanted at all costs to help her mother clear the table, but the mistress said to her, "That's all we'd need! Don't you know what this day means for you? It's the first and last beautiful day in your life, my poor Ginotta. Not even the day when you have your first baby will be more beautiful than this one."

Outside, the groom and his family were already sitting in the wagon, stiffly as though they were offended, but actually it was just to resist the effects of the wine. They had their eyes on the road they'd have to take and had turned their backs on us. I carried out Ginotta's bundle and put it on the plank behind the wagon, but Jano wanted to tie it himself, and since his eyes and hands kept dancing around because of the wine, he tied it so badly that the others would have to get out and tie it again before they were halfway home.

Ginotta had gone up to kiss her father in his bed. I figured her mother had gone upstairs with her and so I went right in the kitchen to grab a few pieces of leftover meat to hide in my straw mattress so I could eat them later that night or next morning. But the mistress was still downstairs, she was kneeling on a chair and praying with her forehead against the wall, and so I didn't feel like it anymore and went back outside.

When Ginotta was sitting in the wagon among those four men, she turned around and cried out to us, "Don't you realize I'm going away? How will you get along without me?"

Jano laughed. "Don't worry, we'll manage somehow."

The marriage broker said giddap to the horse, and Ginotta, who wasn't expecting the jolt, fell back in her seat, but she got up again when they'd already started and called out to her mother, "If I can't come, you come and see me in Agliano! Come and see me at least once a year!"

* * *

Life hands you a load of punishments. Because I waited too long before taking some time off, I never saw my father alive again.

Tobia had already told me more than once that it was time I took my first leave of absence, but I still hadn't listened. It's not that I didn't want to go home for a few days, but I also wanted my family up there to miss me, the way I'd seen them start missing Stefano after he'd been a soldier for quite a while and never came home on leave. And so I held out against my wish to go home, and every day that I could have been there and instead kept hanging on at the Pavaglione made me feel superior. The season, being winter, helped me to hang on, and thank God the work wasn't killing me anymore. Besides, you could spend almost all your time in the warmth of the stable, and that made the food sufficient though there was even less of it than at all other times. But finally the mistress almost got mad at me and said she didn't think I was much of a son, since I didn't feel it a duty to go and see my family after having been away from them for a year, and so I promised her I'd go. It was so certain I'd leave the next day that that evening the mistress said, "When you see your folks tomorrow, tell them we didn't give you the pants this Christmas because of all the expenses we had for our Ginotta, but next Christmas you'll get them for sure." But during the night it snowed again, and I couldn't wade up to my knees in snow all the way to San Benedetto. That day Tobia sent me up on the roof to shovel off the snow.

Then came the feast of us bond servants. The older

ones went down to Alba and a few my age went with them. I would have liked to go along, but Tobia wouldn't let me. His excuse was that Alba was a place full of dangers for young bond servants on a holiday. There were people who'd slip something in your drink and fleece you of what little money you had in all sorts of games, and besides what always happened was that in Alba the older ones would introduce the younger ones to the vice of women by taking them to certain special houses. But he didn't mind if I went to celebrate in the tavern in Manera, which was what those of us who hadn't gone down to Alba had arranged to do. We spent the whole afternoon and evening there. Some bond servants had come all the way from Campetto, and there wasn't much to eat but plenty to drink. For the first time I got drunk like a man, and we even danced, men with men, to the music of an accordion player from Borgomale, for whom we each put up five soldi. That was the very day that my father had his accident.

Three days later, I was on the slope below the house gathering firewood, which was to be my last job before going home. Tobia came and called me from the road, but he didn't give me the news until we were standing on the threshing floor. While I'd been down on the slope, an oil dealer from Liguria, who was coming from my part of the world to the market in Mango, had stopped at the Pavaglione—my mother in San Benedetto had bought some oil from him if on his way to Mango he'd stop and deliver a message for her: to tell me or my master that my father had accidentally fallen in the well, they had pulled him out in time, but he was sick and I should come home immediately.

"I'll never see him again," I said right away, and it was the first time I heard that bell in my ears.

"Don't stand there trying to guess whether you'll see him again or not, just get going."

"You know he's already dead, Tobia, but you don't want to tell me."

"Let my eyes fall out if I've changed a single word of what that oil dealer said. Don't stand there guessing, get going." And he gave me three napoleons as an advance on my year's pay. The mistress said to me, "And on the way pray to our Lord that he let you find your father alive. I'm praying here myself." She already had bread and lard ready for me, and she herself tucked it in my shirt. They all walked me to the gate, one behind another, which made it seem like a funeral already.

I don't wish a trip like that on anyone. It should take four hours but it took me almost six. The trouble was that whenever I talked myself into feeling hopeful, I walked so fast that I got worn out and had to sit down by the side of the road, and while I was sitting there my despair came over me again and I almost didn't have the strength to get up and start walking. I was thinking of the life my father had had, of many of his words and gestures, of Emilio, whether like me he'd been told and was on the road himself, of our mother and Stefano who already knew everything, and I cried and called to my father that maybe it wouldn't have happened if I'd been at home instead of having been sent by him to be a bond servant far away.

I arrived at the village just when it was getting dark, and from above saw our house down there toward the Belbo. It seemed to me that the whole weight of the sky was pressing down on its roof, and it gave me a pang in the heart to see the light in our parents' window, a light that could only come from four candles.

In fact, I never saw him alive again, nor did Emilio, though he'd arrived a couple of hours before me. He'd found a wagon to take him from Serravalle to the Bossola pass.

I stayed a while alone with my father and then went downstairs. I asked my mother if she had any money put aside for the burial, but she told me she didn't even have enough to pay the priest, and so I put my three napoleons on the table. Then Stefano took me to the well and explained how it had all happened: our mother had told him to draw a bucket of water and he had leaned over to free the chain, which had got stuck with the frost. His foot had slipped on the stone and he'd fallen in head first. It was Stefano who'd pulled him out and carried him in the house. He didn't seem to be hurt, but the scare had affected his heart, Dr. Aguzzi hadn't dared to bleed him, and then pneumonia had suddenly set in. Stefano went and got a lantern from the stable and by the light of it showed me where our father's clog had scraped the stone. Seeing it filled me with fear and rage, as though it were a mark left by the devil.

Tired as I was, I was glad, as a little relief from that constant pain, when my mother sent me to tell our relatives about the burial. I did the rounds of Murazzano and Buonvicino, while Stefano had already left for Mombarcaro, Monesiglio, and Sale. Emilio stayed home with our mother. He would see to dressing him and putting him in the coffin. What's more, it was Emilio, the weakest one, who showed the most strength—maybe he'd always had it in the depths of his soul, or maybe it came from what they were teaching him down there in the seminary. "Agostino," my mother said to me in the doorway, "you're the one who's seen him the least. Try to come back soon, before the coffin gets closed." "I've seen him, mother," I told her. "Even if it's already closed when I get back, never mind. I've seen him."

It was sunny the morning of the burial, and I didn't know if this ought to cheer me up a little or make me feel still sadder on account of my father. We brothers were outside early, watching the roads to see when our relatives would arrive. Some came early and some later, all of them with a horse, and of course I went to meet the ones who'd heard about it from Stefano. But the ones I was most interested to see were our uncle and aunt from Mombarcaro, because I hoped they'd also bring their daughter Giulia. Giulia was the most beautiful of our cousins and the richest, the one whose life was the happiest and most ambitious, and the one most often talked about by the rest of the family. I was counting on her being at my father's burial, expecting her to give me special consolation, and when I didn't see her in the carriage with her parents my heart went down to my shoes. As though I still didn't believe it, instead of going to greet the others, I followed Aunt Emilia and Uncle Annibale into the house and heard my mother ask her sister why she hadn't brought Giulia. "But how could I?" replied Aunt Emilia. "You know very well that my Giulia is in Mondovi studying with the nuns."

By now they'd all arrived. They kissed each other on the cheeks, saying, "It's only at times like this that we all get together." They sat down and waited for coffee. Our mother served it, saying the same thing to everyone: "Oh, what I've been through." And then she had to send me out to buy a little more coffee.

You could tell by the looks and movements of the relatives that it seemed to them the time would never pass, while for me it was racing by. Uncle Annibale pulled out his silver watch and asked why the bell hadn't started ringing for the transporting of the coffin. Emilio went to find out and came back saying that the priest from Costalunga was late, he had sent word that he refused to come on foot, and that if they wanted him in church, they'd have to send an animal. Uncle Annibale offered his carriage, but Emilio said that Canonica had already gone up and our mother blessed Canonica: "Who would ever have said it at the time we were fighting over the store." "Poor Melina," Aunt Emilia said to her, "if you only knew how easy it is to play the good samaritan after you've won."

Already people were whispering outside and trampling the snow, and through the window we could see the yellow of the Carmelite sisters, which was our mother's order. Then Canonica must have arrived with the priest from Costalunga because the bell started ringing for our father.

Four men lifted the coffin, hoisted it on their shoulders, and carried it outside, with all of us behind crying, and the one who cried the loudest was Stefano, with his handkerchief over his mouth. As for Emilio, he didn't cry because he had to recite the rosary along the way, and I could hear that his voice was quite steady.

In the church they speeded things up because they had the last mass to think about. The altar boys were there and when the three priests didn't need them, they scuffled with each other, picked their noses, and stood for some minutes trying to get a good look at our relatives from the outside world. I'd done the same thing myself, but at that time I didn't know I'd ever be in the front row behind a coffin.

When we came out of the church the weather had changed—the sun had gone into hiding and in its place there was a cold wind that fluttered the pall on the coffin, and once we were outside the village blew out the tapers of the Carmelite nuns. We stopped so they could relight them, but the wind blew them out again and so we went on without them. By eleven o'clock he was buried and I'd aged ten years. We walked back slowly. Our mother was waiting for us on the threshing floor with Aunt Emilia, who was holding her by the waist. "Is it all over?" she asked. "Have you done all you could for the poor man? After dinner I'll go and see."

For dinner there was tuna, sardines and olives, chicken and its broth. Our father had had to die to put us under the obligation of serving such a meal. If people at first were still silent, it was because they were all hungry, but then they got warmed up and started talking. They talked about the deals they'd made or were thinking of making, about prices and brokerage fees, and at a certain point Uncle Annibale said loudly that they owed him fifty thousand lire in the Bormida valley. Aunt Emilia said right away it wasn't true, but he said still louder, "It certainly is true, and they're going to owe me more!" We ourselves took part in their conversations, asked questions and answered them, and when they laughed we managed to smile. One by one, they all asked Emilio a lot of questions about the seminary in Alba, but nobody asked me anything because I was a bond servant, the only one in the family, and it embarrassed them too.

It was already late for the season when we got up from the table, just looking out the window at the sky gave you a chill in your spine, and you could see by the faces of all our relatives how they hated having to make their way home over those rugged *langhe*. Our mother wanted to serve another round of coffee, but they wouldn't let her, and as soon as they'd kissed us one by one on the cheeks they got back in their wagons. The last was Aunt Emilia, who said to us brothers, "Look after your mother. Take good care of her and above all see that she eats. And if she doesn't want to and says she doesn't feel like it, you must force her, just like with geese." She was one to talk—being the owner of a store, bakery, and butcher shop, she had all of Mombarcaro in her pocket and ate so well she had a neck the color of ham.

For supper we had polenta and quince jam. Then Stefano said like a baby that he felt sick. He went to bed, and our mother went upstairs to take care of him. I instead went out in the cold, got to the cemetery, and started walking up and down along its low wall as though to keep my father a little company. I heard footsteps in the snow. It was Emilio who'd come with the same idea, and we threw ourselves in each other's arms and cried on each other's shoulder.

When I look for some fact that could give a picture of my father and our clan, the first thing that comes to my mind is how he met and married our mother. But it would be better to hear it told by Netino, the way he told it to Emilio and me the last time we were with our relatives in Monesiglio for the feast of Saint Biagio.

When he was about twenty years old, my father had been away from home for quite a while, waiting on tables for his Uncle Pietro, who kept the inn in the square in Monesiglio. He stayed almost two years, until he had to go back and work the soil in place of his brother who was leaving for the army. But he wanted to take home a woman from Monesiglio or thereabouts, because at the time he'd left there wasn't one he liked in all San Benedetto, and he was sure the right one hadn't turned up in those two years. And so he spent his last months in Monesiglio looking for her, in all the families where he was invited and without missing a single dance. But he didn't find anyone because he was too hard to please, at least that's what Pietro's son Netino said—he and my father were as close as two twins.

One day when they were sitting on a bench outside the inn, Netino said to my father, "Last night I heard it strike two and you still weren't back. Where did you end up?"

"At a dance at the Colombis. I left with the musicians."

"And did you find anyone?"

"Nobody."

"I can see you still won't have tied the knot when you go back to San Benedetto."

"I wouldn't keep looking if I wanted the queen of Sheba," said my father.

"You're too hard to please."

"But here it's a question of mingling blood. You're too quick to say I'm hard to please."

Netino had nothing more to say and started gazing at the houses across the square. Then all of a sudden, as though he'd found a napoleon in the mud, he said: "Melina!"

"Melina who? Biestro's Melina?"

"Of course, Biestro's Melina. Why do you go looking over half the Bormida valley when all you have to do is cross the square? How come you never thought of Melina?"

She was a daughter of those Biestros who had a thriving cheese business. She worked with her brother on the other side of the square, and maybe he'd never thought of her because he'd never heard any man mention her. She was as tall as my father, sort of severe-looking, and ever since she was a little girl she'd always dressed in black. Nobody had ever seen her at a dance. She went to church but without drooling over it. One strange thing about her was that she rode a horse like a man, she'd go riding all over the Bormida valley selling her cheeses, and for that she wore soldiers' leggings. Because of those leggings, there were people in Monesiglio who thought she was crazy.

"So do you want her?" said Netino.

"I'd take her, but what about her?"

"Go and find out."

"And if she says no?"

"No man ever dropped dead because a woman said no."

"Let me think about it until tomorrow."

"What d'you mean think about it, tonight you'll sleep with Melina under the pillow." And Netino crossed the square, took a look through Melina's window, and came back. "Go ahead, she's inside packing cheeses."

"I'm not ready."

"How aren't you ready?"

"I don't know what to say."

"But you've got a mouth that doesn't shut up even in front of the priests. Go ahead, change your clothes, put on your good suit."

Pushed and prodded, my father went, in his Sunday suit but with last Sunday's beard, which he only realized when in front of Melina he touched his face with his hands.

Melina had turned away and was stooping over to put her cheeses in a basket. He didn't give her time to turn around. "I'm Giovanni Braida," he said all at once, "Pietro Gavarino's nephew, and I've come to find out if by any chance you'd want to marry me and come and live with me in San Benedetto."

She half turned her head and here's how she answered him: "Don't you think I know who you are, you who celebrate carnival every year there in your village of San Benedetto?"

"But I'm not joking, if that's what you mean. It's not carnival time for me now."

"Listen, Braida, I'm all upset today because one of the Bragioli women came to bring me her cheeses and I paid her for twelve and now I see there are only eleven. It's not the best moment for jokes."

"But who's joking? Not me. I'm standing here waiting for you to give me a serious answer."

Then my mother stood up, came toward him, and she was as tall as he. "If you're not joking, I won't say yes or no just now. But come back when my brother is here. He's gone over to buy in Torresina."

My father went back to the inn, gave himself a good shave, lent a hand at serving a table of cart drivers, and when he heard Biestro's horse, he went back to the house across the square. "My sister Melina has told me all about it," Biestro said to him. "As her brother, I'm glad, because I know you're a good fellow, with your little piece of land in your own village, and here in Monesiglio you have good kinfolks. But you'd better go and see our father and mother and declare yourself all over again to them, and whatever answer they give you will be the right one. You know where they are."

Their house was on the other side of Black Roads, where we went twice, when our grandmother died and later our grandfather. The two old people were sitting at the table but weren't talking to each other. The old woman's head drooped and in the rare moments when she held it upright she looked cockeyed at her husband. Like everyone else in Monesiglio, my father knew why her head drooped, and there was nothing unusual that at that hour she was already soused since it was after dusk. Wine they'd taken away from my grandmother, but they often found her drunk anyway, until they discovered she kept a supply of Fernet in the chamber pot.

My father repeated his request, more at ease now because he'd already passed one test, and the two old people listened to the end. "All right," Biestro kept saying, "all right, all right"—as though he had to give some kind of answer to someone who was talking to him about the wind and rain. He took out a cigar and stuck it in his mouth, but while my father was striking a match for him, the old woman like a cat snatched the cigar from between his teeth and hid it her lap, covering it with both hands. My grandfather swore once, but ended by just saying to her, "That's a fine trick you've played on me, whore, you've shown off to Braida with a very fine trick." Then he said to my father, "All right. The same as for our other three daughters. Because me and this old woman here, we've brought four daughters into the world, as you'll find out, and three already have families, and one of them has even taken a sea captain from Savona, you'll find that out too. Well, everything just like for the other three. Melina's time has come too. What we did for the other three we'll do for Melina, and gladly."

The old woman got up, holding onto the table as though she were standing on the edge of a cliff, but Biestro made her sit down again, and asked her what she wanted to get up for.

"Coffee for Braida. Let's at least offer Braida a coffee, he's taking Melina away from us."

"You don't have to get up. Call the maid."

My grandmother called the bondmaid and then asked my father, "You'd like a drop of Fernet in your coffee, wouldn't you?" My father drank only wine and said no. "But don't you know that a drop of Fernet in your coffee helps settle your stomach?"

"Since when does a man like Braida need to settle his stomach?" my grandfather said harshly, and he looked at my father to see if he'd understood why the old woman kept talking about Fernet. My father had come to another conclusion, and he was afraid that since he hadn't agreed to the Fernet, he'd never be able to get along with his mother-in-law.

They drank the coffee without the drop of Fernet and afterwards my grandmother started crying and calling out, "Melina, Melina, Melina!" Then all of a sudden, she got up, went to the door, opened it, and screamed outside: "My Melina's getting married, my Melina's going away!"—and fell down the whole flight of steps before the two men could do anything about it.

It didn't take a minute to realize that even with my father gone, I wasn't needed anymore at home. We didn't have a penny to our name, and were at the mercy of the slightest misfortune. He'd left us between six and seven *giornate* of land, and a man of Stefano's age and build could work it all by himself. What was needed at our house were the seven napoleons a year that I earned down there at Tobia's, as Stefano told me plainly, in a voice that sounded as though he were surprised I was still there and hadn't already packed my bundle again. The same with Emilio. "You go back to the seminary," he told him. "We'll do what little we can for you, but you'd better go down there and study hard so you can sew on those black buttons soon and take our mother with you into the church they're going to give you."

I don't know about Emilio, and anyway he'd always had less to do with the house, but as for me, being ordered around by Stefano put me in an anxious state of mind, it was almost a warning that I was going to be cheated. Stefano had ordered us around before, after all there were five years' difference between him and me, who was the second oldest, but over him there'd always been our father. Seeing him now with all the power in his hands didn't leave me feeling exactly calm. Not that Stefano had any big vices, but ever since he'd come home from the army, I didn't trust him anymore, I saw him as being out for himself. Or maybe he made me so suspicious because everything had been a disaster. I'd seen what could happen when I was away from home.

I'd hoped, though I knew they couldn't do it, that with our father's death, my family would let me stay home from now on. And later I'd hoped, if it was my written destiny to work for others, that my uncle and aunt would call me to Mombarcaro, where between store, bakery, and butcher shop they always had need of bond servants. But on the day of the burial Uncle Annibale didn't say so much as a word to me about it, and I didn't dare bring up the subject with him. Now I've come to understand that you don't take on your relatives, at least if you want to stay on good terms with them.

My mother's silence decided me even more than Stefano's words. She didn't often look at me and whenever I was able to look her in the eyes, she seemed to be saying:

"Resign yourself and go back because I'm already resigned to having you far away."

What's more, I had Tobia to worry about. The day after the burial I was already wondering when Tobia was expecting me back at the Pavaglione—having left the way I did because of the accident, we hadn't had time to decide on what day I was supposed to be back. And it was something to think about, because now it was Tobia I had to set my hopes on, after my illusions of being allowed to stay home or else being called to Mombarcaro by my uncle and aunt. And so, between Stefano and Tobia, I ended up going back on Wednesday. I spent the whole day before lying in bed and crying now and then in anger and grief, because I knew what was waiting for me at the Pavaglione, knew it exactly by days, months, and seasons, and in those few days I'd been home again, despite the mourning, I'd broken the habits I'd made during more than a year at the Pavaglione, as happens with anything you do for a long time without putting an ounce of heart in it.

There was nobody around the Pavaglione I could call a friend, but I didn't have any enemies either, except maybe for one crazy character who with no provocation from me and just to be funny had lit into me one feast day in Manera, but it didn't go beyond words. By now I knew a lot of people, and almost all of them I'd met inside the walls of the Pavaglione, because Tobia's house was the chief place to gamble in those parts. Baldino, the younger son, had the magic touch with cards, Tobia had let him have the pack and he wouldn't let go of it, wouldn't even lend it to Jano, or let him play a practice game with me. On gambling nights, Baldino would take out his pack of cards—nobody in the house knew where he hid it—and spend half an hour shuffling them without once looking up, until the young fellows from the neighboring farms came knocking at the door of the stable, and after a little horsing around to hide their impatience, they'd start cutting for *nove.* Tobia would squat behind Baldino and study the game over his shoulder, laughing out loud when Baldino uncovered his top card, and giving him a little slap on the neck whenever he raked in the kitty.

I pretty soon lost what little I had and would go and sit on the straw, partly to watch the others playing and partly to watch the mistress spinning in the corner. Jano was like me at cards and always had bad luck, but unlike me he had the illusion that he could make up for it, and when he'd lost everything, he'd ask Baldino to lend him some of his winnings, but Baldino would never lend him a penny, and in this he was backed up by Tobia who made bets on the game and knew his older son to be a loser.

Speaking of gambling, even up where we live it's an inborn vice and they play hard, especially in Murazzano, but there's no comparison with the lower *langhe*, where in a single night farms of sixty *giornate* are won and lost, and where they turn out such expert gamblers that they go all over the world, known by name in the gambling houses of Alba, Asti, and Turin, and who even go and gamble in France. I've actually seen a man from Lequio who won a million at Monte Carlo. He'd stopped at the Manera crossroads, wearing all new clothes from his hat to his shoes, and he had his winnings in a little package hanging on his finger, a little package like the ones they make in Alba to wrap sweets. All the people from around Manera came running to see him as though he were an attraction at a fair. He waited until a small crowd had gathered, then raised his finger and showed the package of money around. "I can buy everything I see," he said. "Oh, you good people, I could make you all my tenants." He was a man from Lequio.

If it hadn't been for the card games, maybe I wouldn't have met Mario Bernasca. He was the best player besides Baldino, and his natural opponent, but he let him win nine evenings out of ten, and I who kept rooting for him felt bad about it. But he himself didn't seem to care, and after he'd lost everything he'd brought with him always said good-naturedly, "Anyway it's not mine, it's what I won during the week." And it must have been true, because he never lost less than a scudo and he couldn't have had that much if he hadn't won it at *nove* or *bassetta* someplace else. "So, Tobia, don't charge us for the light tonight," he'd say when he'd lost a lot. But Tobia always insisted on collecting a fee for the light, even when Baldino had had a winning streak all evening.

I remember a night when Bernasca had already lost more than two scudi and Baldino was laughing like a she-ass when they bring her to the male. The mistress stopped spinning—she was scared for Mario and ashamed that her son was winning so much. "You'd better quit, Mariolino," she said to Bernasca, "or this'll be the evening when you lose a month's pay."

I looked at Tobia and saw the scowl of anger on his face. Bernasca, however, drummed his fingers on the wood and said, "I'm not quitting, I want to see if your son is the devil." "Quit, Bernasca," she said to him in a tone of command, "otherwise next time I won't let you in."

Tobia jumped up from the straw, and for a moment we all thought he was going to hit her. Instead he only cursed and called her two or three names to her face, and so she gathered up her things and left. Then Tobia said to us, "Just remember, you young fellows, women are animals.

You can't catch them because they don't have tails, but if you hit them on the head they feel it." And he went back to his place behind Baldino. But this time things didn't go the way he wanted, because Bernasca, having seen the way the mistress was forced to leave, stopped playing for that evening.

I felt drawn to this Mario Bernasca, and I had the idea he wanted to be my friend too. But we were never anywhere but among a lot of people at the Pavaglione, and there was never a chance for just the two of us to talk. The first time he spoke to me, he said, "You and me, we're a couple of idiots," and he said it as he went past me to go in the stable and play cards. Another time he said the same words to me and I didn't understood them any better than before, but I couldn't get offended because he included himself among the idiots.

He was my age, but had a whole different outlook. He wasn't even eleven years old when his family had sent him out as a bond servant for the first time, and no one had seen so many troubles. Bernasca was willing to tell his story in company, and a greenhorn bond servant once asked him didn't his family have any heart. "Does my family have any heart?" he replied. "You know what my father said to me when I made a fuss? 'I've supported you this long,' he said, 'now, God willing, your arms will work for you the way your mouth has done since the day you were born. Get going, I don't feel any more sorry for you than for a winter sparrow.' " He said loud and clear that he hated his father, and that for him the worst day was when his father came up from Barbaresco to collect the year's pay. My mistress, who didn't like to hear such talk about a father, once told him that if he was his father he could only be a good man, but he laughed in her face and said, "You'd have to taste my father cooked in oil to find out how good he is."

If Tobia hadn't kept me on a chain the way he did, I would have gone over one day to see Mario where he worked as a bond servant. He lived on the other side of the Chiarle rock, an hour from us, with an old couple, man and wife, who owned a two-room shack with a stable and a small plot of land, but it was he who did all the work. And so for months, much as I wanted to talk to him, I had to be satisfied with knowing that as far as Mario was concerned, the two of us were a couple of idiots.

Fortune didn't stop smiling on the Rabinos. The years may not have been bountiful but they were good, and neither the animals nor the family ever felt the touch of hard times. As for my master, I'm the only one who knows all the things that Tobia managed to put by. So my pay was never in danger, but already it wasn't enough for me—by now I was giving Tobia a good return on his investment and was worth something more than the seven napoleons a year agreed on with my father. Now that my father was gone, it was up to me to make Tobia recognize what I was worth so that my pay would increase the way it ought to. I'd still send seven napoleons home, but keep the rest so as to be able to show off once in a while like Mario Bernasca. But I was too polite and never got up the nerve to speak of it directly to Tobia. I had what I wanted to say all set in my mind but kept postponing, and since

I was convinced that I'd be staying at the Pavaglione for all eternity, I felt there was plenty of time. And anyway Tobia would someday in all conscience have to speak to me about it himself. Of course, he never brought up the subject, and finally I was the one who spoke up, one time when I wasn't even thinking about it, but was angry over an example of his injustice. He'd ordered me to salt the water for the animals and I'd salted it, and then he denied ever ordering me to do so and chewed me out about it. I defended myself as best I could, and then since I'd already gone that far, I mentioned my pay. He started yelling for all he was worth, and it was a good thing his two sons weren't around because otherwise they'd have come out and beat me up as though I were skinning their father alive. He yelled that we were all out to suck his blood, that I had no business asking him to raise my pay just because I'd seen the year go by without storms or frost, that eighteen-year-old shitheads were now breaking the agreements made by men of sixty, and he ended by saying I could pack my bundle and vacate the straw mattress for that same evening, that he already had someone else to take my place for much less, and thank you very much.

To have to go away on foot and look for a place to sleep like a tramp scared me, and left me unable to argue in my own interests. Tobia, realizing he'd got the better of me, cooled off and said we'd talk about it another time, but only after the harvest. And he left me there in the middle of the threshing floor. I'd accomplished nothing and maybe only given him one more reason to treat me harshly.

The mistress, who'd heard our angry voices from inside

the house, came up to me and said, "Be patient, Agostino. That's how my husband is. If you say 'take' to him, he understands it at once, but if you say 'give me,' he doesn't even hear. I'm going through it myself."

"I know," I said, looking at the ground.

"But you don't know everything. Since the day Ginotta left, I've had you four men on my hands. And I tell you it's wearing me down, and who knows if I'll be able to hold out."

"How do you feel?"

"For now just tired, but very, very tired."

"You ought to rest."

"And who'll look after you four? I need for Tobia to get me a bondmaid, but I don't even dare ask him. We must all be patient, Agostino. I know, you're not a member of the family and so you have a right to be impatient, but be patient all the same. I can tell you what's gnawing at Rabino's brain. A great fear of not getting where he wants to be before they call our son Jano to the army."

It's a fact that the second year was much tougher than the first. Young as I was, I started walking bowlegged like someone who's been digging with a spade all his life. Jano and Baldino were all bent and twisted too, but I was only looking at myself, who besides didn't have the compensation of owning anything. There was the same amount of food as before, except to me it always seemed less because my body was growing and so was the work. It was during that time that I stole the salame. I'd never been so hungry or had such an opportunity, with no one in the kitchen and on the table a butt of salame that the mistress may have been thinking of breaking up and putting in the soup, and the dog off his chain for once and sniffing around the door stoop. I ran inside, grabbed the salame and tried to stuff it in my shirt, when out the window I saw Tobia coming across the threshing floor. I felt so lost and in the wrong it was as though I'd killed someone, and gulping down the salame whole, I got out of there fast. What saved me was finding the dog underfoot, which gave me an idea. Yelling thief and murderer, I sent him running with a kick. Tobia believed it, and when he had the dog on the chain again he beat him so hard he almost killed him and then gave him nothing to eat for two or three days. But that salame, between having swallowed it in such a hurry and the scare I'd had, did me no good.

You get to a point where you can't help having illusions and go looking for help where there's not even the shadow of it. I mean that having realized by now that to Tobia I was nothing but a beast of burden with the handicap of speech, I was looking for an opportunity to get on the good side of the Pavaglione's owner, who was even higher than Tobia—or at least be noticed by him. And I made a stab at it once when he came up to get away from his pharmacy for half a day. He'd remembered the dog and had brought him some meat wrapped in paper, which would only have needed a little roasting on the fire and I and even Tobia's sons would have gobbled it up.

Having taken a look at the fields, he'd come back to the porch and was talking to Tobia. I started circling around and when I heard they weren't talking business anymore, but about the wind and rain, I got closer still. I was just two steps away from him and waiting for the right moment to butt into the conversation with something that might please the landlord, when he turns his head and says to me, "Get away, a person could faint from the smell of your sweat."

If only I'd just had my own miseries, but I was also worried about Emilio, and without my brother coming into it directly. It was the young priest from Trezzo who made me anxious. One morning when I was at the well drawing up pails of water like the beads on a rosary, he showed up on the threshing floor and asked me to call the mistress. I knew him from having seen him at Ginotta's wedding, and because he was the one who always made us stop playing football on feast days and sent us off to vespers, and I called her outside.

"Would you have any work to give me," he asked her, "anything at all, just so the day I bring it back to you I can be sure of getting some bread and cheese to eat?" And in his voice and manner he was like those peddlers who go from one farm to another, though he looked more miserable. But she treated him as a priest, and said, "I'm afraid I really have nothing, Don Pino."

He shook all over from head to foot. "Are you sure there's nothing broken in the whole house? For instance, does your alarm clock work? Because if it doesn't work, I could fix it for you."

The alarm clock worked all right, I could have told him that.

"Not even a chair that needs a new straw bottom?"

I could see the mistress hesitate. If it had been only up to her, she would have helped him right away, but she was afraid of Tobia. In the end, however, she told him she could give him her chair to fix, the one she used for spinning in the stable. I brought it out myself, and the priest looked it all over from top and bottom and then said it was worn out, with the legs all eaten away, and if she liked he'd make her a new one. But the mistress couldn't go that far and to get rid of him she went to get him a loaf of bread, and she herself stuck it in the pocket of his cassock. The priest put his hand over it and said, "Believe it or not, but I've got to the point where I'm thinking of learning to play the clarinet so as to earn something on feast days."

We stood there watching him leave with the chair on his shoulder, and that day I realized that young priests are a little like us bond servants. They're lucky or unlucky depending on which parish priests they draw, exactly like us with our masters.

"I feel so sorry for that poor Don Pino," said the mistress. "The old priest lets him starve because he himself is used to eating little or nothing and doesn't care that this one is young and with an empty belly. There's plenty for two in the parish, but the old one spends all the money building a wall around the property. Even between them, there's misunderstanding and unfairness."

This was what made me worry about Emilio, that after all that effort and sacrifice away from home, no sooner would he have sewn on his black buttons than he'd end up like this Don Pino. The only priest I'd known fairly well was our parish priest in San Benedetto, and while it's true he ate very little and not only on Fridays, he wouldn't have been able to complain about it with a clear conscience, and he was the one I thought of when I tried to picture Emilio's future in the church. But after this business of the parish priest in Trezzo, I who now saw everything in the worst light couldn't get rid of the idea that my brother would have the same fate as this Don Pino.

A whole month went by and then finally Tobia took me down to Alba. This time we went without the cart and all he brought along was his wife's shopping basket. The first thing I did was to go to the seminary, walking halfway across Alba but with little eye for the city.

At the seminary, Emilio looked even worse than the first time. You saw mostly his eyes, and his neck was no bigger than that of a six-year-old boy, from what I could see under a black woolen scarf that I never knew he had. I asked him if it had come from the seminary, but he told me our mother had brought it to him. She'd come to Alba a month and a half before, in Canonica's wagon, and as long as they were traveling over the *langhe*, she'd sat on the seat, but at the sight of the first houses in Alba she'd moved back and crouched inside a big basket, out of shame and fear of the city.

I started to say, "How stupid of our mother, how stupid," but meanwhile my eyes were looking around that room where she'd been a few Saturdays ago, and I was in such a daze I didn't answer my brother. I was startled to hear him cough, a dry, hacking cough that made him hold his chest with both hands, to which I didn't pay enough attention though it should have put me on the alert from that time on.

"I'm just glad winter is over," he said, "because I was sick and tired of breaking the ice in the washbasin every morning."

"But can it really get as cold as all that in here?"

"You won't believe it, but it's colder in here than on the Mombarcaro hill on Christmas night."

"What's new with you?"

"They've put me in the choir."

"You must be glad. It's an honor, isn't it? And are there benefits to being in the choir?"

"But I'm tired, Agostino, and every morning when I wake up, it's all I can do to get out of bed. When you're this tired, even singing gets to be too much. After class, the ones who aren't in the choir can rest, but we have to go to the chapel and rehearse." And he added, maybe on purpose to change the subject, "But you folks in San Benedetto would stand there with your mouths open if you could hear the things we sing."

But I didn't let him change the subject. In fact, all his talk about tiredness and sacrifice had reminded me of Don Pino's story, which I told him in so many words.

When I'd finished, he smiled and said, "I'm not worried about what may be waiting for me afterwards."

"If I were in your shoes, I'd start worrying from now on. Because it'll be your profession for the rest of your life, and I'm telling you it's not all roses."

"But how do you know I'll even get to be a priest?"

I took this to mean that Emilio wasn't doing well in that kind of school. Even I knew that you can flunk out of the seminary just like out of our elementary schools. So I asked him how his studies were going, with all that Latin. Having never had anything in my hands but a hoe, I was sort of embarrassed in talking about these things, but after all he was my little brother.

Emilio actually laughed. "I didn't mean Latin. That's not what scares me. I'm in the top half of the class."

I understood so little that I didn't even feel like asking him to explain what he meant. He had gone to sit down on a bench, under a portrait of the bishop, and from there he asked me if I'd come down on my own.

"No, my master is waiting for me on the other side of Alba."

"It's nice of you, Agostino, to come all this way just to see me."

"I'd get up from a wedding feast to come and see you. If only I could see you for once someplace besides here. Couldn't the two of us spend half a day together, outside in Alba when the weather gets a little warmer, in the public gardens or even along the Tanaro?"

"They only give permission to the ones who are lucky enough to have relatives in Alba. But maybe we can see each other at home and take a walk along the Belbo, but for the whole day, and we'll take something to eat with us. Try to get your master to give you some time off when I'm home on vacation."

"I can see you're not from the country anymore," I said. "When the time comes for your vacation, I'll be up there harvesting, first the wheat and then the grapes."

Like the other time, we heard bells ringing inside every five minutes, and they kept interrupting our conversation, until the right one rang and he had to run off. First we kissed each other on the cheeks and I left him a lira so that once in a while he could buy something to cheer himself up.

I found Tobia where we'd agreed to meet, but instead

of starting back for the *langhe* right away, he took me with him to see the landlord, not at his home, but in his pharmacy. It's the one on Via Maestra, on the way to the cathedral, with gold snakes painted on all the windows, lined inside with shiny old wood like the choir of our church in San Benedetto, and with the shelves full of jars that many wedding couples in our parts would be very glad if they were to have one in their bedroom.

Our landlord was out from behind the counter, standing and talking to a friend of his sitting in the light near the window. They were discussing hunting rifles that cost God knows how much. Tobia begged his pardon and said we'd just stopped by to say hello and see if there was anything he needed from the Pavaglione. While the landlord was asking Tobia if up where we were it had rained like in Alba, a woman came in with a prescription. The landlord went behind the counter and prepared the little package for her, and you should have seen the way that woman bowed and scraped to him even though she was bringing him a profit. "Some business," Tobia whispered to me, "some business he's got his hands on." The landlord took the woman's money and stuck it in a little machine that from a distance looked like silver, and when it had the money in its belly it went dring! Tobia and I both pricked up our ears.

Then Tobia took the landlord aside, but I could still hear what they were saying. "She's been complaining for a long time now," Tobia told him. "But I don't think she's faking it, she really doesn't feel well."

"What is it she feels?"

"Maybe it's some kind of inflammation, I don't know,

but she complains at all hours of the day and night, and she's even put verbena on her stomach."

Tobia should never have mentioned the verbena. The landlord got mad and raised his voice. "Ah, so she's put verbena on her stomach! Did she at least put it on by the pitchfork? I'll bet a hundred to one she went to that healer in Villaio."

"No, no, it must be something she knew about herself."

"Some knowledge!" The landlord turned to his friend and said, "You see the kind of heads we have on the *langhe* when it comes to practical matters?" And the man nodded, as though to say he also knew what sort of people we were. Then the landlord turned back to Tobia. "But can't you tell me anything about how she feels, so I can get an idea from here what's the matter with her? First of all, is she still menstruating?"

"I really don't know anything about her ministrating."

"Does she stoop over when she walks?"

"I guess so."

"Does she hold her sides?"

"Yeah, I guess so."

"Tobia, your wife is worn out. It's time you took on a bondmaid for her."

"A bondmaid costs money."

"With three napoleons and an apron at Christmas, you can do it."

"I can't."

"I know you can."

"Whether you know it or not, I can't," Tobia answered sharply, not at all like a tenant to a landlord. There was nothing like the subject of money to turn him into a man.

"I'd like to see you do your accounts after you've buried her," the landlord said.

"But is she as worn out as that?"

"Never mind. Next time I come up, I'll take a look at her."

"We'll be waiting for you. And when are you coming up?"

Instead of the landlord, it was that friend of his who spoke up, and said, laughing, "It would be some smart landlord who let his tenants know beforehand when he was going to come and see them."

The landlord laughed too, and even Tobia said to him cheerfully as we left, "So long, boss." But as soon as we were out in the street, he said to me, "Did you see that machine that goes dring every time you put money in it? I wish I had one, and the boss's money to put in it. Just to hear it go dring every five minutes. A scudo—dring! Another scudo—dring!"

You could say that even after the gambling season was over I never stopped seeing Mario Bernasca, but always in company, and then for days thereafter I'd think about the words he threw at me on those occasions. There was nothing exact about them, but they promised that sooner or later we'd have a good talk face to face. And it happened that one Sunday afternoon, he came up to the Pavaglione and called me to go with him for a swim in the Belbo. From inside the house I asked him if anyone else was coming with us, and when I heard him say no, I figured the time had come.

We were sitting on the bank in our underpants, after we'd helped each other dry our backs. Mario spoke:

"I keep telling you that you and I are a couple of idiots. The fact is we're wasting our youth being bond servants, and under such lousy masters, when it seems to me we've got the strength and brains to go it alone. And so why don't we start out on our own? Why couldn't we be harvesters, for instance? Haven't you ever thought of that kind of life? The owners go down to Alba and hire them, they bring them up and later take them back in a carriage, and if they don't have one they rent it because it's the harvesters who set the terms. And they have to give them what they want to eat, if they want hot sauce the owners have to give them hot sauce, and meanwhile they can fool around with the women of the house because anyway next day they're someplace else. In one day they put in their pockets anywhere from fifty soldi to three lire, and next day they start all over again at some other farm."

"But the grain gets cut only once a year," I said.

"But there's plenty to do afterwards. I know that harvesters have their work cut out for them until the fall, and still on account of the grain—for at least two months they have to transport the grain to the station in Alba. Maybe you've never talked to these harvesters who come up from Alba, but the other summer I talked to one of them who'd been hired at the Rustichello, and I asked him so many questions that he finally told me to shut up, but meanwhile I'd found out a lot of things. Well, that one had his work guaranteed until October, and still only with the grain."

"But what about afterwards?"

"So afterwards it's all over, that'll be great. You've got a pocketful of money, and there's plenty of work for people like us down there in Alba. It's all work that our hands can do, because when you're a bond servant in the country you learn how to do a little of everything. In Alba we could set ourselves up as bakers or butchers, their assistants I mean, or even as stablemen."

I let him go on talking, and stared at the water so that Mario wouldn't see by my eyes that I didn't have the courage to take the risk, and that not even he would ever be able to give it to me. But he sensed it, and said suddenly, "Don't you feel brave enough? Are you one of those people who think they have to die on the *langhe* just because they were born there? Or are you afraid that if you start living your own life you'll spend all the money you earn and won't be able to send anything home?"

I started to say that this might also be a reason.

"Don't be a sucker," he said. "Think about your folks at home, because they've already thought about you. The best they could do was send you out to be Tobia's bond servant."

I resented this a little and said, "I don't know how you feel about your folks, but I'm not bitter toward mine. And anyway that's the sort of person I am. I've never had any luck, and I'd have a hard time finding a friend if I went all over the *langhe*, but I don't feel like being a tramp. At Tobia's I sleep on a straw mattress, but when the day comes when I don't know where I'll sleep that night I'll be a lost soul."

He got mad. "And do you think, stupid, there are no

straw mattresses in Alba? If things go well, there'll be beds for us in Alba." He stared around so as to be able to turn back to me with a less angry look, but he was more riled than ever when he said, "I've never had any luck either, just like you, but at least I don't go around pretending to be a good son."

No wonder Bernasca kept getting madder. I was sitting there with a blank look on my face and talking more like a child than a man, while he had a fire under him and the need to hear a definite word from me. But I couldn't say it to a lone wolf like Mario, since to me, leaving aside courage and the sort of person I was, keeping my place at Tobia's was as good a way as any of preserving the memory of my father, who had put me there before he died, and of salvaging the respect of my family, who at least would always know where I was day and night.

But now he played all his cards and told me to consider another angle. "If after the harvest things don't work out in Alba, we haven't lost anything, because we can always go back to being bond servants."

"I can't wait to see the kick in the ass I'd get from Tobia."

"That's where you're wrong," he yelled, "that's your little mind! For you nothing exists but Tobia, the sun rises and sets on the Pavaglione. You must be crazy if you think we'd come back to work on this *langa*, where the soil gives the masters an excuse to treat us like dirt. We'd go and work someplace else—in the Diano valley, if possible. There's a fellow from my village who has the luck to be a bond servant in the Diano valley, and I talked to him once. You should have heard him, and I'll bet anything he was telling the truth, he wasn't just saying it to make me envious. Apart from the soil being softer, there's the attitude of the masters there—compared to them, ours are disgusting and deserve to get hit on the head with a hoe. There the masters give each bond servant a couple of eggs on Sunday to exchange at the store for enough tobacco to smoke for the rest of the day, they let you invite your friends to their wine cellars, and not to mention the wine, there's always a big basket of bread and a jugful of pickled peppers. It's like having Christmas all year round. And there the farms are big, really big, and it's nothing for all of them to have five or six bond servants. So you see there's nothing to worry about if we don't make it in Alba. But I'm sure that after a couple of months we'll be doing fine in Alba."

He'd been sitting next to me the better to persuade me, but when he saw he'd made a mistake in relying on me, and that I kept making excuses to get out of it, he got up, walked four or five steps away, and yelled that he'd go by himself.

"When are you going?"

"I'll go. I'll show everyone on this *langa*, I'll show you first of all."

We went back up. Everything between me and Mario Bernasca was finished before it had hardly begun. He didn't even stop by the Pavaglione, but took a shortcut across the slopes to leave me and avoid it. I got back to the house with a look on my face that must have made Tobia smell a rat, because that evening he said to me, as though for no particular reason, "He's good as gold, Mario Bernasca, but he's got no more brains than the jack of spades." I said nothing. I couldn't stand Tobia that evening, even less than usual. My head was full of those masters in the Diano valley.

Down there on the banks of the Belbo I'd thought that Bernasca had taken an interest in me because he liked me, and wanted to improve my lot along with his, but that same night I figured instead that he'd done it because he didn't have the courage to run away from the *langhe* and seek his fortune in Alba by himself. In any case, after that Sunday, I avoided him whenever I could, because even in company I felt uncomfortable with him, worse than if I'd owed him money.

If they still remember me in those parts, it's only because I was the one who found Costantino from the Boscaccio.

Those people at the Boscaccio were a breed who held their heads so high they never knew if the ground was dry or wet, they all thought it best not to be seen on the threshing floor, not even to help husk the corn, and when they were right people were all agreed in saying they were wrong, and when they were wrong it was just their nature. Although it was the farm closest to the Pavaglione, we never did anything together. They weren't on speaking terms with Tobia because of something Tobia had done to Costantino at a time when I didn't even dream I'd end up as a bond servant at the Pavaglione. All the local farmers were celebrating a feast in Montemarino, and Costantino had brought his accordion, but just as he started the first song, Tobia, who was already drunk, picked up a pair of scissors that happened to be lying there and punctured the bellows. His companions made him settle for two scudi, but since then they hadn't spoken to each other.

One day the rumor spread that Costantino was missing from home. I remember the mistress saying right away, "He's a brute. He told his wife once before he was going to kill himself, just to frighten her and make her cry." "But this time," said Tobia, "just because he didn't say anything, this time he's really gone off to kill himself. It's a chain. His brother did it, they found him hanging from the rafters more than twenty years ago. Costantino's already held out for too long." Then Jano said, "Maybe he went down to Alba and jumped in the river. He wouldn't be the first one," and after Jano, Baldino wanted to have his say, but the mistress made him shut up because this wasn't a matter for children, and besides she wasn't feeling well and it upset her too much.

Day and night, all over that *langa*, you heard nothing but people calling Costantino, and at any moment when someone didn't have anything else to do, he'd give out a yell. The family turned loose the dog, which had a special love for its old master, and the sons kept following it around in case it found him, but the dog, which had been tied up all year, led them all the way past Le Grazie only to find a bitch. Meanwhile people, each one on his own and without telling anyone, had already sounded their wells, and you can imagine how horrible it was for me with my father's accident still fresh enough in my mind.

We were already pretty sure that Costantino had gone off to kill himself and had our feelings about it all ready, and so we were a little sorry when we heard that he'd been seen in the tavern in Campetto eating bread and sausage and carrying on about everything and everybody. His youngest son rushed over to Campetto, but none of it was true. That evening they kept the church in Cappelletto open on purpose for anyone who wanted to pray for Costantino, that he be found alive, and the mistress went, but Tobia shook his head. To him it was all a waste of time and breath—at this hour Costantino was already feeding the worms. And I have to admit that Tobia was right.

To Tobia all this fuss about Costantino was a pain in the neck because it disturbed us in the fields and made us unwilling to work. Often we'd straighten up and look across at the Boscaccio's threshing floor, and we envied people who could take time off from their work to stand there for hours waiting for news. We had to wait until evening to catch up.

One morning a man from Rocchetta arrived at the Boscaccio and told the sons that he must have seen their father, but it was already a week ago. "I saw him at the market in my village," he said. "Someone was telling about a man he knew who'd hanged himself that week. Just as he finished, a man who was surely your father joins our group, he puts his hand on the shoulder of the one who'd been talking and says, 'He had courage, that friend of yours, he had courage.' And then he went away, I don't know where."

All of them just stood there and after a moment the oldest son asked what this was supposed to mean. "It seems to me it tells the whole story," answered the man from Rocchetta. Well, everyone had to hold the oldest son back to keep him from strangling the man instead of offering him a drink, in exchange for having traveled up and down three hills to put them on their father's trail.

Costantino had been missing for seventeen days, when we at the Pavaglione found ourselves without a handful of bran, and the closest place where Tobia could borrow some was the Galla, which is halfway between the Pavaglione and Trezzo. I went to the Galla, loaded my sack, and was slowly making my way back when I had to answer a call of nature. But there were two girls in the pasture nearby and no matter how far off the road I went they could still see me. It was only a few steps more so I decided to go in a grove of oak trees, growing so close together it was like entering a small room, and as I ducked under the first branches I found Costantino's feet against my stomach. It was him all right, even though I wasn't able to look him in the face—the highest I got with my eyes was his chest, where he'd pinned a piece of paper with writing on it.

It was something just to have had the strength to get out of there and not fall down like dead under Costantino's feet. I went back up on the road without touching the ground, yelling and waving my arms so much that those two girls didn't feel like waiting for me and ran away, the sheep ran away too, and even the birds disappeared in the sky. To the men in the distance I yelled two or three times that I'd found Costantino hanged, signaling to them by putting my hands around my neck, then I fell back and sat on the road and started vomiting. I couldn't stop, it was as though my ass were in my mouth.

People came rushing up, all they asked me was where, and I pointed with my finger to that grove of trees in hell.

When they came out they were all holding their noses like there was an awful stink, but I hadn't smelled anything. They told me later that I must have had the wind in the other direction. One by one, they came and put a hand on my shoulder, saying, "What a horrible dish to be set in front of you, young man." Tobia came too, and I asked him what was that piece of paper Costantino had on his chest, which had looked to me like somebody's written revenge, but instead it was the souvenir of the Shrove Sunday mass in the parish church in Trezzo, and according to Tobia, Costantino must have thought of putting it over his heart in the hope that our Lord would partly forgive him. I also asked if he'd been dead for only a little while, but Tobia said he already had more worms in him than a rotten cheese.

By this time Costantino's sons knew all about it and arrived with their cart. They wanted to load their father on it and take him directly to the Trezzo cemetery, since he'd killed himself closer to the cemetery than to his house. Tobia and the other old men stopped them, calling them crazy, and wouldn't let them lay so much as a finger on him until the police sergeant from Neive had seen him as he was.

Tobia was pissed off because I was wasting time waiting for the sergeant to ask me questions, and he was also afraid of losing another half day if the matter wasn't cleared up and the captain should have to come up from Alba. But he made Jano and Baldino carry home the sack and stayed to back me up while I answered the sergeant.

Although I was the one who'd found him, I hadn't seen him as well as everyone else, but I never let on that I didn't look at his face. When I told my adventure—and they made me tell it a hundred times—I was helped for the details of the tongue and eyes by what I'd heard from the others.

Then Tobia got his first box on the ears. One evening a little before suppertime, instead of calling us to eat, the mistress all of a sudden gave a loud cry and then screamed that she was losing blood. When we were all in the kitchen, she told us she didn't have the strength to go on or even to get to the bed by herself and lie down. Her three men carried her up, while I stayed at the bottom of the stairs, but then Baldino yelled to me that they needed light and so I carried up the lamp.

There was a woman-smell stronger than the smell of the potatoes spread out on the bricks, and Tobia at that moment was shutting a drawer where a handful of linen had got caught in the middle.

"Did you see, Rabino?" said the mistress in a voice that sounded to me as though she were dying. "I've kept going, going, going, but now I can't go on anymore. You didn't want to get me a bondmaid, and now you see what happens."

"You never said anything to me about getting a bondmaid," Tobia said.

"Because if I'd said anything, you would have called me all kinds of names and probably beaten me up. But what kind of man are you if you can't see that I needed a girl to keep things going? You've always used me as if I were an iron machine, but now you can see I'm nothing but flesh and blood."

He leaned over the bed and said to her, laughing, "But are you afraid you're going to die?" I'm ready to swear that he laughed and spoke that way with good intentions and only to cheer her up, but she took it for a sneer, and lying there flat on her back started slapping his lowered face with both hands. Caught by surprise, he did nothing to defend himself, but then he stood up and moved a few paces back from the bed.

The mistress felt herself a little under the blanket, then she pulled out her hands and put them over her eyes, and like a blind woman, who must have lost any idea of who was in the room, she said, "Sure, now you'll get me a girl, now that you've ruined me. You started ruining me from the very beginning. Remember the first time I had to give birth? It was my first and you knew very well that the first one is never easy. Nossir, you made me slave away when I had only one more day to go. Always remember, Tobia, you made me work on the hay when I was already losing fluid!"

Jano was squeezing his head between his hands as though he wanted to pull it off and throw it away, he turned completely around, then stopped in front of Tobia and shouted, "Sonofabitch of a father, I'll kill you with my bare fists!"

While the mistress started screaming, Tobia said to Jano, "That's a fine way to behave, a boy like you hitting an old man like me," but as he spoke he bent down to the potatoes, and when he stood up again he had a sickle in his hand. "Now, you bastard," he yelled, "let's see those bare fists of yours!" and threw himself at Jano. Though no one had bumped against me, I dropped the lamp, and

Jano escaped by running between me and Baldino, both of us petrified with fear, and with Tobia after him with the raised sickle. The mistress had the strength to scream but not to lift her head, Baldino was stammering, and I, when I heard them get to the bottom of the stairs and run through the kitchen, dashed to the window and saw Jano running away alongside the house, while Tobia stopped in the doorway and lowered the sickle. I went over to tell her that Jano was safe and had made it to the woods. After crossing herself, she said, "Tell Tobia to unlock the cupboard for you. There's lard, cut yourself a good piece, so at least you'll have some supper."

But I didn't dare approach Tobia just to talk to him about eating, and besides the scare had put my stomach to sleep. Never before had I been so close to seeing blood spilled, and anyway when I went downstairs I couldn't find Tobia. Baldino walked past me but didn't stop, he went to stand near the pear trees and think his own thoughts. I could have gone to the stable, but it was a nice evening and I wanted to enjoy at least a moment of it, so I went around the house to stretch my legs in the darkness on the Mango road. But behind the house, I immediately saw Tobia. He was sitting on a log against the wall, right under the window of his and the mistress's room. He was holding his head between his hands and talking to himself, but I couldn't hear anything of what he was saying because the breeze carried his words away. After a minute he raised his head and spoke out loud, but loud like someone who wants to make himself heard all the way to the *langa* of Castino over there on the other side. "Listen," he said, "I've never crawled on my belly, not me. Everyone knows I lead a better life than the priests. I've driven myself as much as you, only I never talk about it, and if something happens to me, I keep it to myself, no matter how bad it is. What do you think, has it crossed your mind that I'm sixty-two years old, and I work so hard I'd lose more than blood, if I had a hole too to lose it from! And since you talk about the hay, do you know what it means at my age to cut hay from sunrise to sunset? Anybody can cut hay when they're young like your sons and the dew is on it, but when the sun is high and the hay starts giving off dust, that's when the hay asks you how old you are! So there, if it's all because of the hay!"

He sat there as though waiting for the mistress to answer him from their room, but nothing came from her. Instead, up from the slope, came Jano's voice: "Murderer, murderer, you're a murderer!" Tobia went to the edge of the slope and yelled down, "I'm telling you one thing, just you try not showing up for work tomorrow morning. That's all I have to say to you." We all waited for Jano to answer, but he didn't let himself be heard again from down there. Instead, Baldino on the threshing floor started yelling to silence the dog, aroused by Jano's angry voice in the distance.

Tobia went and sat down on the log again, and I could hear him clicking his tongue to get his saliva flowing after all that yelling. Then, in a lower voice, he said, "You all take me for your slavedriver. But you know why I work and make you work and don't give you anything more than necessary. And even if I fail in my plans, you should still thank me for teaching you how to suffer today so as not to suffer worse tomorrow. And don't come and tell me you can't suffer any worse than this, because it wouldn't take much for me to show you the opposite. Suppose I told you about someone whose father died when he was a boy and he was taken in by his uncle, over there near Cravanzana. He made him work so hard that by comparison you're a bunch of country squires, and at noon he'd tell him, 'I'll give you two soldi if you don't eat dinner,' and he had to take the two soldi, and when it was time for supper, 'If you want to eat supper, you have to give me two soldi.' You know I was that boy? You people have never known what it's like."

From above came the mistress's voice, telling Tobia to go to bed, since he'd been on his feet since daybreak, but that first he should eat something, drink a raw egg. "How long has it been since you've tasted an egg, you poor miserable man?"

I felt sick at heart and went to the stable, thinking of what goes on in families and wondering if our mother, in remembering her dead husband, would have to make room in her memory for things like this.

My hunger wouldn't let me fall asleep, and I was still awake when, it must have been around midnight, I heard the stable door open. I reached out for the pitchfork, but then came Jano's voice: "Agostino, are you awake? Move over a little, tonight I'm going to share your mattress."

The bondmaid arrived sooner than expected. She came from the *langa* of Castino and was even a relative of Tobia's, but a branch of the family that had fallen on hard times. Her name was Fede and she was about eighteen.

Since I was really stuck on this girl, you might think

that even now I'm making her out to be better than she was, and yet the truth is she was a girl full of refinement, who knew how to look and act better than all the girls we were used to seeing. She could stand at the stove for hours and then turn around as clean as if in all that time she'd been nothing but a lady, she walked in her clogs without ever making them clatter, and her voice had more than one tone, like the voices of women in Alba. But with all her grace, you had to see her at work and the comfort she gave the mistress, who had soon made peace with Tobia when he found and hired her. And just when you thought she'd finished doing everything, she sat down at the window in the twilight and started mending stockings, there's no counting all the stockings she mended for us. I'll always remember that the rare times when she made a mistake she had the habit of sucking in her breath as though she'd pricked herself with a needle, and then you'd hear Tobia say, "Be more careful, little whore." She always ate standing up, as she'd been taught to do by her family with the idea of making her a bondmaid, since masters are happier if their servants eat in a hurry.

Young as she was, she'd already seen plenty of trouble, half of which would have been enough. She had three brothers, but two were already dead, both from typhus and one after the other—Fede's family had figured out too late that the dung heap was too close to the well. And then she had an older sister, but with tuberculosis, and I had an idea it was because of her that Fede hadn't minded being sent out as a bondmaid. Her sister was dying but too slowly for her mother's patience, and Fede couldn't stand to see how she treated her, and she herself not being able to speak. By now her mother did nothing but snort and say to anyone who showed up, even if it were a tramp in the doorway: "I'm so fed up always having to feed her separately and then wash her stuff right away, always having to do everything for her separately, that I'll be glad when she dies. But it looks like she's taking forever to die."

Now Tobia's sons and I knew what to do in the afternoon. We no longer left the threshing floor, and would wait for her to come out and empty the dishwater or set the soup bowls out to dry in the sun, in case something nice could be seen when she made some movement, and you can be sure we wouldn't have missed it because not one of us three so much as blinked an eyelash. The day she'd arrived, Tobia wanted to have her sleep in the kitchen in the corner by the stove, but the mistress always let her sleep in her room—she piled up the potatoes and spread a straw mattress for her. Not even during the day did she lose sight of her, because she knew what she was up against. I'm thinking of the time she caught her younger son in the stable with the sow and the beating she gave him with a strap on his bare ass, and in all his pain Baldino could only bawl, "But when we kill her this winter, will we find a baby inside?"

But Fede treated me nicely, and I for my part was always on the lookout to see if I could give her a hand with anything, and this from the very first day. One evening we were husking corn and half the young people from around there must have been on the Pavaglione's threshing floor. Tobia orders Fede to make the rounds of those who are thirsty, which she does, serving everyone with water and vinegar, but to me she gives wine. Right away I started wondering what sort of sign this could be, and I went quietly around the whole company asking each one what Fede had given him to drink—she'd given wine only to me, and that gave me a lot of ideas and great hope. Unfortunately the evening ended badly for me, and it wasn't her fault but all Jano's, who once we'd finished husking and had started singing and making jokes, stuck an ear of corn between his legs and leaping like a ram chased Fede for five minutes until she had to call for help from the mistress. That's all that was needed for me to start dreaming of the day when Jano would have to leave for the army, and I hoped that everything Tobia was doing to have him declared unfit would fail. I was quite happy the evening when Tobia came back up from Alba and said that our landlord the pharmacist couldn't do anything for Jano at the military hospital in Savigliano. And I was also glad that Mario Bernasca had left, because Mario had plenty on the ball and for all I know he might have made an impression on Fede. And while I'm on the subject, I'll tell how he escaped from being a bond servant, because Bernasca had a certain importance in my life at that time.

Mario Bernasca did what down on the bank of the Belbo he said he'd do—he disappeared one night without letting anyone know. Next morning his master and mistress got the idea that having run off like that, he must have had something sticking to his fingers, and in their anxiety they blew the horn, which really gets blown only when livestock is stolen. All the farmers rushed to the valley to block the road for the thieves, but they had a hard time finding the tracks of any animals and beating all the bushes. They shouldered their rifles and told the old man from the Chiarle rock to resign himself and forget about his animals. Only then did the old man explain that there were no animals missing from the stable, but that it was all because of his bond servant Mario Bernasca, who'd run away in the middle of the night and taken things with him. Everybody, especially the younger men, started talking about Mario as if he'd done nothing but steal ever since he was born, until somebody asked what it was he'd stolen. The old man got all confused and said he didn't know exactly because he hadn't yet had time to count his possessions. Then they got mad at him and called him all kinds of names, though he was old enough to be their grandfather. That was the end of it, and no one has ever seen Mario Bernasca in those parts since. But we found out later that when he ran away he was clean as a whistle—his master had sent him over the day before to the bakery in Manera, and while the bread was baking the baker's son had plucked all his feathers in a game of *nove* on top of the oven.

Since I'd seen how Jano, one time when we'd all gone to a feast in Trezzo, had bought Fede a bar of nougat candy and she'd willingly accepted it, I put aside a little money and the next time I went down to Alba I bought her a little bottle of perfume for twenty-five soldi at a booth in the square. And with that little bottle deep in my pocket I went to see my brother at the seminary, but this time I didn't leave him anything to buy himself something to eat because all my money had gone for Fede's present. At home, I buried it in my straw mattress and waited for a chance to give it to her. I could have put it in her hand at a moment when no one was looking, but I wanted to have the opportunity to speak to her a little. But I could never manage to corner her, because whenever I didn't have the eyes of Tobia and the mistress on me, I had those of their two sons.

Fede always treated me well and looked at me more sweetly than at the others, but this wasn't enough for me anymore, and besides I'm the sort of person who'll spend all tomorrow wondering if something that seems sure as death to me today is true. And by now her favoring me with wine instead of water and vinegar was ancient history. One thing that, while it annoyed me a lot, somewhat confirmed my ideas about Fede was that now when Jano was around her he treated me with contempt, as though to make her see the big difference between himself and me, and he almost kept watching us at the table as though he were afraid we'd speak to each other with our eyes. What's more, he often talked about Fede to his brother loud enough on purpose so that I'd hear him too, and he said things that may have been compliments for Fede as a woman but which hurt me inside.

But one fine evening I was able to take her aside, an evening when Tobia and Jano had gone to Torretta to get the advice of a private landowner whose son the year before had been in the same situation as Jano and who'd been able to have him declared unfit. As for the others, Baldino had been sent to the bakery in Manera, and the mistress was looking after the rabbits, which were the animals she liked best. I went around the house and looked in the grating of the kitchen, and I stood there stock still and so silent that Fede when she turned around got frightened as though she'd seen a ghost.

"What do you want?"

"For you to come outside."

"What for?"

"To talk a little."

"We can talk where we are."

"I don't like it here, it smells too much of your Rabino relatives."

"But I have to cook supper."

"Well, I have to take care of the animals."

"We must be crazy!" she said, but she came out and I took her not far away, where we could even hear the mistress's voice a little. I wanted us to go behind a hedge, but she said no, someone might go by and a girl who accidentally lets herself be seen with a man behind a hedge gets immediately criticized, rightly or wrongly. So we sat on the edge of the slope, and to put myself on her right I jumped down and passed in front of her—she put her legs together right away and crossed her hands on her knees. Then I sat down next to her and told her she was really a nice girl but that with me she didn't need to be so much on her guard.

"I could see right away that you were a nice boy," said Fede. "So what is it you want to tell me now that I'm here?"

"Well, lots of things. One of them is I'd like to meet your folks, and for you to meet my mother, who lives in San Benedetto."

"There's nothing wonderful to see at my house."

"So you wouldn't mind leaving it."

"But still they're my folks."

"I meant, do you ever think of getting married?"

"It doesn't matter how a woman feels at home, that's what she's made for."

"You too?"

"Why not? If I find somebody who wants me."

"And what should he be like, that man?"

"Nothing unusual. So long as he's not lame, not hunchbacked, and doesn't have red hair. Most of all, so long as he works hard and doesn't hit me for no reason at all."

"My bad luck not to be a man yet."

"But you're a man already. I can tell, you know, by the work you do."

"Would you trust me?"

"Very much, if you're always the way you are now."

"And would you like me as a man?"

"I like you as a man."

"I'm so glad to be at Tobia's!" I said. "If anyone had told me a few months ago. And you, are you glad to be at Tobia's?"

She was glad too, and now I would really have been stupid if I'd started wondering about the reason for her joy. Slowly I said to her, "There are some tough jobs around here I could take."

She knew immediately what I meant. "That's how we'd have to start," she said. "With lots of patience and good will."

"One thing you can be sure of, the job will be more scared of me than I of it."

"That's just the reason I trust you."

"So, Fede, girl, will you leave it to me? And when I say the word, will you be ready?"

"I'm happy and I'll be ready. All you have to do is speak." She stood up and said, "My supper."

I followed her toward the house, and I was even out of my mind with all that good luck. One more step and all of a sudden I felt scared at having good luck for once. "Wait, at least tell me when it was you decided."

"Those aren't things that happen on an exact day," she said, without turning around.

"It wasn't by chance that time when you gave me wine and everybody else water and vinegar?"

She stopped. "Don't be silly," she said, as though she'd had a little weakness and I'd guessed it. But then: "Still you're smart."

At the gate I asked her again if some evening in nice weather we couldn't be alone together where no one could see us. "But how could we? Let's be patient, Agostino, and you'll see afterwards we'll be even happier because we waited."

In ten minutes we'd been able to say everything to each other and make arrangements for life, and that conversation was worth months, worth all the times we hadn't been able to speak except with our eyes, but I don't think we were unhappy at having to keep it secret, we were so sure of ourselves.

Now I wouldn't have left the Pavaglione for anything—as long as Fede was there it was the most wonderful place in the world. And now Sunday was always a real holiday. Every Saturday night I shaved what little beard I had, and every Sunday morning, on the way down to Cappelletto for mass, I walked with the other men behind the women, and each time I could smell from Fede's hair the perfume I'd given her.

Jano hardly gave me any more trouble, because now he had troubles of his own. That man in Torretta had explained that the reason his son had been declared unfit was that for three months before the medical examination he'd beaten his knees with bags of sand, a little each day, until they swelled up like two balloons, and so the military doctors at the recruiting hall down in Alba had told him to get dressed and go home. Tobia wanted his son to do the same treatment on himself, but Jano was afraid of being deformed for life and never found the courage to begin, and when Tobia got mad because time was now short, he started crying like a baby.

For me instead everything was going perfectly. There was so much strength and youth and joy in me that I now did twice as much work, and Tobia even felt embarrassed and promised me a reward of three scudi, to be given to me after the harvest. This meant I could cut somewhat more of a dash and give Fede some pleasure, like the time I took her to Cappelletto to see the magic lantern of that man from Roddino, and for two soldi each we saw a fox hunt and a woman chasing her husband with a broom.

I didn't even want to hear about taking a leave of absence, and I'm not ashamed to say it, my only thought for my family was to hope they were all still alive—even Emilio seldom came to my mind and then only for a moment. My thoughts were only for myself and Fede, and as soon as I had an hour free I ran over to the tavern in Manera, where there was always a certain coming and going of people, and tried to find out as much as I could about the tough jobs to be had. I must have listened to a dozen people, the ones who knew the most, and they all told me the same thing—for a year's work they paid a hundred lire, a quintal of corn, and a cask of wine. Convict labor, but nothing daunted me and I wouldn't have turned up my nose because of the place, when the time came I would even have accepted a job under the Cissone rocks. With Fede beside me, I was sure I could succeed in anything, in my small way, and that luck would be with me always, no matter in what place I started.

Time flew by and all of a sudden it was Christmas. Tobia and the mistress kept their promise this time, and took Fede and me to the market in Alba to make me a present of a pair of pants and for her an apron. I remember it like it was yesterday. At a booth in the cathedral square the mistress chose me a nice pair of striped trousers and made me try them on over the ones I was wearing, and you should have seen how Fede, who already had her apron rolled up under her arm, discussed it all with the mistress and the clothes seller and how she checked to see if they fit and tried to find defects in the cloth. Just as though I were already her man.

And instead nothing came of it. One rotten evening her father and brother arrived on foot at the Pavaglione and went into a huddle in the kitchen with Fede and Tobia and the mistress. After an hour they went back where they came from, but taking Fede and her bundle away with them. She left with her eyes cast down, and as she walked past me she bowed her head still more. What was I to think, except that her sister must have died or was in her death throes? As soon as I could, I asked the mistress, but she only said it was a family matter of Fede's—she'd guessed what there was between the two of us and probably didn't want to give me a stab in my heart. I was the last to find out that one of the Busca brothers from Castino had asked to marry Fede, and her family had rushed up to get her for fear of losing the match by an hour's delay, because now their Fede would be making a rich marriage.

"Do I know them, these Buscas?" the mistress had asked Tobia.

"You saw them at my cousin Vica's funeral, but maybe you don't remember. They're three rough customers, ugly as sin, with no woman in the house, but they own the best piece of land at Castino."

I stood there like a calf after the first blow with the mallet. Nobody will ever make me think she'd been pulling my leg and only wanted to pass the time while she was there as a bondmaid. Instead, taken by surprise, always used to bowing her head and without me beside her who might have given her the strength to rebel once and for all, for fear of being tied to the leg of the table and beaten with a strap until they finally dragged a yes out of her, that's how she must have given in, and as for me she would have figured I'd be a little mad at her but then I'd get over it and look for another girl. Now I've almost got over it, but for a long time I felt that having lost Fede, I'd lost the whole race of women.

You never saw a wedding take place so fast, not even if Fede had slipped and there'd been a baby on the way. They got married at Castino, the first Sunday in February.

Tobia and the mistress were invited to the wedding and went, taking two towels as a gift. Jano and Baldino could have gone too, and I would have been able to be alone for a day, which was what I wanted and needed. Instead I had them on my neck the whole day, making jokes, and they even meant to do a *porrata* on me, which means scattering a trail of leeks and corn to the door of someone who's been jilted by a woman the day she marries someone else. But they only talked about doing it, because that's the day they would both have got skinned alive. Only toward dusk was I able to be alone for a while, with my eyes staring at the Castino hill, which had more lights than usual, and with my memories and plans lying useless in my hands like empty boxes.

Tobia and the mistress came back next morning, and he was still so full of everything he'd seen that night that he took up the whole road. The minute he reached the threshing floor, he spread his arms and started crowing about Fede's good fortune—only two weeks ago she'd been our bondmaid and now compared to her the rest of us were a bunch of beggars. But I heard the mistress say to Tobia a little later while they were resting by the fire: "You know something? I'm afraid those two older brutes got the youngest one to marry Fede so that all three of them could use her. Poor girl."

That evening I skipped supper. I didn't want anyone to see that I didn't even have the strength to chew.

Well, in the middle of ruin and with life now unbearable for me at the Pavaglione, where I couldn't take half a step without bumping my nose on something that reminded me of Fede, the wheel made a turn and I had a stroke of luck, the first in the twenty years I'd been in the world. Our uncle and aunt in Mombarcaro, with so much money they didn't know what to do with it, and unable to spend the rest of their lives enjoying themselves like gentry, opened a new store in Monesiglio, and for their first assistant, they sent for my brother Stefano. Stefano couldn't wait to leave the land, which had become too low for him to stoop over, and as for me, it was my dream to go back home and work it myself.

I gave Tobia a week's notice and he could hardly believe it. He was sure it was all a trick of mine to get away more cleverly than Mario Bernasca, but luckily I had Stefano's letter to show him, and so Tobia let me go and paid me what he owed me. That was certainly a bad day for him because, though it's not for me to say so, he wasn't about to find another bond servant like me right outside the gate.

I packed my bundle and said my goodbyes, especially to the mistress. Afterwards I didn't look back, not even where the road goes down from Benevello and you lose sight of the Pavaglione. The nearly three years I'd spent there I'd already forgotten, almost as though they were a penance.

I made that trip back as though it were the most wonderful thing in my life. It was my real feast day, and at Arguello I stopped at the tavern, ordered a bottle of muscatel and drank it all to celebrate. I felt I was coming back like a soldier, not from the standing army, but actually from a war. The only shadow in all that sunshine came when my eyes wandered toward the *langa* of Castino.

When I came in sight of San Benedetto, I set my bundle

down in the middle of the road and swore an oath never to complain even if I had to stay there and live on nothing but bread and onions till I was dead and buried, just so long as I never had another master. Then I went down to greet my mother, and for her too it was the first good day in God knows how long.

The house was falling apart. The whole roof needed to be fixed, the wall on the Belbo side was bulging out like the belly of someone with water sickness, and there were so many holes in the windowpanes that a wolf could have come in, not to mention the wind. So I'd also have to get busy as a bricklayer and carpenter. The land too had to be completely retilled, you could see from a mile away that Stefano had hardly scratched it. But now I'd make it feel my hoe. It was enough that I was working for myself the way I'd worked under Tobia, and with a little luck and my mother helping me out with her cheesemaking, we could hope in time to lift ourselves out of poverty, and if things went right for a few years, I might even be able to buy back what my father had had to sell.

The first mornings, I had one big worry. The first thing I did when I got up was to look out the window to see if my fields were still there, if a landslide hadn't buried them on me during the night, as I heard had happened to people over in Cissone and Somano. Those few *giornate* meant there would never be another Tobia in my life, and as for Stefano, I would liquidate his portion as soon as I could. I was already dreaming of the day when we'd go to Dogliani together to sign the deed.

Little by little I found out all the things that had happened while I was away. The worst was that we no longer had the woodyard. To make ends meet, my mother and Stefano had sold the rest of the woodyard, and during the winter they heated the house with wood that Stefano would go out at night and steal. Finally the owners, the Ghilardis from the mill, set up an ambush, jumped him while he had an armload of wood, beat him up, and left him there more dead than alive. My brother was in bed for almost three weeks, but nothing reached the ears of the police sergeant in Bossolasco.

I still get chills in the spine when I think how we'd reached the point where a puff of wind would have been enough to make us lose both land and house, leaving us with nothing but our arms outstretched to the world. And if things had got any worse, Emilio would now have to die of other things besides his disease.

Last Saturday we were at the seminary down in Alba, my mother, myself, and our parish priest, having been sent for by the rector. Emilio had done something really crazy. After class, he had run ahead of his companions and been the first to arrive in the refectory, where he'd taken a bite out of all the loaves of bread that were already on the tables and then locked himself in a latrine, and to get him out they'd had to break down the door. His superiors had had him examined right away by their doctor and they found he had tuberculosis, which he'd already had before entering the seminary. All we did down in Alba was receive the news and they asked my mother questions about whether there'd ever been others in our family. She and I stood wringing our hands like when a storm batters the fields, and then the doctor started explaining to my mother all the things she'd have to do when she had Emilio at home again. Our priest took me aside and said that unfortunately there was no force in the world that could save him—if there'd still been a ray of hope the priests would have sent him to their hospital instead of home to die in the bosom of his family.

You can imagine if we've let slip a single word, and yet all of San Benedetto knows about Emilio's sickness, and some women have already come to the house to console my mother and give her support.

Emilio is supposed to arrive on Saturday evening with Canonica's wagon, which will be coming back from the market in Alba. In my heart of hearts I still hope he'll be saved, saved by our air and our food, but this evening without meaning to I overheard my mother praying. For fear I was in the house and might hear her, she went outside and knelt down by the first stake in the vineyard. By chance I was in that row, looking to see how an apple tree was budding, and I heard her say: "Don't call me until I've closed the eyes of my poor son Emilio. After that you can call me if you like, whenever you want. And then consider what I've done for love and be indulgent with me for what I've had to do. And all of us who'll be up there, we'll hold our hands over Agostino's head, because he's good and has sacrificed himself for the family and will be all alone in the world."